First published in 1991 by Grisewood & Dempsey Ltd,
Elsley House, 24–30 Great Titchfield Street, London, W1P 7AD.

© Grisewood & Dempsey Ltd 1991.

Designed by Cathy Tincknell.
Cover design by The Pinpoint Design Company

ISBN 0 906279 54 2

Printed and bound in Italy.

ACKNOWLEDGEMENTS

The Publishers gratefully acknowledge permission to reproduce
the following copyright material:

Joyce Gillham: for *Naughty Daisy* from "The Read-Me-Another-Story Book" edited and
compiled by Dorothy Edwards, reprinted by permission of Methuen Childrens Books;
Anita Hewett: for *Kangaroo Joey Finds His Shadow* and *Elephant Big and
Elephant Little* from "The Anita Hewett Animal Story Book", reprinted by
permission of The Bodley Head; David L. Harrison: for *The Giant Who
Threw Tantrums* from "The Book of Giant Stories", reprinted by permission
of Jonathan Cape and the author; Stephen Gammell: for *Wake Up, Bear...
It's Christmas!*, reprinted by permission of William Heinemann Ltd
and Lothrop, Lee & Shepard Books, a division of William Morrow & Co. Inc.

Stories adapted from traditional sources are as follows:

*The Bell of Atri, Hedgehog's Waistcoat, The Frog Prince, Five in a Pod,
The Day the Sky Fell Down, The Clever Little Girl and the Bear,
Why the Raven has Black Feathers, Saint Patrick and the Snakes,
The Big Turnip, Billy Bear's Stumpy Tail, Goldilocks and the Three Bears,
How Crab Got its Hard Back, The Months of the Year, The Best Thing To Do,
The Mayor's Egg, Titty Mouse and Tatty Mouse, Master of All Masters,
Nail Soup, How Ishdaka Found Summer, The Gingerbread Man,
The Happy Spinner, Sweet Porridge, Hare the Hero, Beauty,
Thunder and Lightning's New Home, Teeny-Weeny, The Three Billy
Goats Gruff, The Old Woman of the Forest, Pulled Out of the Water,
The Cock, the Mouse and the Little Red Hen, The Elfin Knight,*
and *One at a Time* are adapted by Nora Clarke.

Polly and the Buckets of Milk is adapted by Neil Drury.

The Husband Who Looked After the House and *The Frogs Who Wanted a King*
are adapted by Deborah Manley.

The Hazelnut Child, The Three Brothers and *The Cat and the Mouse*
are adapted by Peta Rée.

The Publishers would like to thank Nora Clarke for her kind
assistance in the making of this book.

Tick Tock Tales

3

Minute Stories

Illustrated by
Annabel Spenceley

Edited by Sian Hardy

WHSMITH
EXCLUSIVE
·BOOKS·

CONTENTS

THE BELL
OF
ATRI

In the market place of a little Italian town called Atri, there was once a high tower with a bell. The bell had a long rope that dangled down to the ground. When the king had ordered the bell to be hung in the tower, he had said, "My friends: everybody here can reach the bell-rope, even the smallest child. If ever anything goes wrong and you need help, I want you to pull on the rope. I hope you won't pull it very often!"

Now the people in Atri helped each other all the time, so the bell had not been rung very often – only five times so far!

One day, as the king was riding by, he saw that the bell-rope was very thin.

"Dear, dear," he said to his wife, "the rope is getting old. We must get another one at once."

"The rope was made in a faraway village," said the queen, "I'll send someone to get another."

"Yes, do that," said the king. "But suppose somebody wants to ring the bell in the meantime?"

"What about fastening that grapevine to the bell?" replied the queen. "It is very long and it should last until we get the new rope."

"What a good idea," said the king. And the grapevine was fastened to the bell immediately.

Near Atri there lived a rich old man. He had once owned many horses, but he had sold them all, one by one, until at last there was only one left. For many years the man rode everywhere on this horse. Then, one day, when he visited the stables, he said to the horse, "You're old and you can no longer work. You're no good to me any more. Why should I feed a useless horse?" And he drove the poor horse out of the stable and locked the door behind him.

The miserable horse walked along the road looking for some hay or grass to eat. But there was none to be found and, as the days went by, he grew thinner and thinner. At last, one afternoon, he tottered into the market place of Atri. He stopped by the grapevine with its fresh, green leaves and happily began to munch on the lower leaves. When he had

9

finished these, he tugged at the grapevine to reach the leaves higher up the vine.

Ding-dong, ding-dong went the bell. Everybody rushed out of their houses to see what was the matter.

"Why is the bell ringing?" asked one man.

"It's that poor old horse pulling the vine," exclaimed a young boy.

"I know that horse," the man said. "He belongs to the old fellow who lives in that big house not so far away. He must have been turned out because he was getting too old to work."

"What a shame," said a woman. "We should take that mean old man to see the king."

Well, when the rich old man was brought before the king, the king was very angry.

"This horse was a good friend to you for many years," he said, "but now you have thrown him out like rubbish. I order you to take him back, give him a warm stable with plenty of hay and feed him properly."

The old man's face went bright red as he led his horse away. The people of Atri cheered loudly, and you can be sure that the horse was well looked after to the end of his days.

HEDGEHOG'S WAISTCOAT

A hedgehog and a mouse once lived happily together under a thick hedge. One day, the mouse found some juicy pears and she brought them back for supper. Now the hedgehog was a very greedy fellow and when suppertime came, he ate one pear, then another, and another until his stomach got so big that his waistcoat popped open!

The mouse felt sorry for the hedgehog, so off she ran to the shoemaker and said, "Shoemaker, please give me a needle and thread to mend Hedgehog's waistcoat."

"I'll give you some thread if you bring me some eggs from Hen," said Shoemaker.

So Mouse ran to the hen and said, "Hen, please give me some eggs for Shoemaker. Then he'll give me a needle and thread to mend Hedgehog's waistcoat."

"I'll give you some eggs for Shoemaker if you bring me some corn from the farmer," cackled Hen.

Mouse ran to the farmhouse and said, "Farmer, please give me some corn for Hen. Then she will give me some eggs for Shoemaker and he'll give me a needle and thread to mend Hedgehog's waistcoat."

11

"I'll give you some corn for Hen when you bring me a nice apple pie," said Farmer.

Mouse ran to Baker and said, "Please bake a nice apple pie for Farmer. Then he'll give me some corn for Hen, who will give me some eggs for Shoemaker, and Shoemaker will give me a needle and thread to mend Hedgehog's waistcoat."

But Baker said, "I'll bake you a pie if you bring me some milk from Cow."

Mouse ran to Cow and said, "Please give me some milk for Baker. Then he will bake an apple pie for Farmer, who will give me some corn for Hen, who will give me some eggs for Shoemaker, and Shoemaker will give me a needle and thread to mend Hedgehog's waistcoat."

And Cow said, "I'll give you some milk if you bring me an armful of rich green grass."

So Mouse ran to Field and said, "Field, please give me some of your lovely green grass for Cow. Then she will give me some milk for Baker, who will bake an apple pie for Farmer, who will give me some corn for Hen, who will lay some eggs for Shoemaker, and Shoemaker will give me a needle and thread to mend Hedgehog's waistcoat."

And Field said, "Of course you can have some grass. Take as much as you want."

So Mouse took lots of grass and ran back with it to Cow. Then Cow gave her some milk for Baker, who baked her a tasty apple pie for Farmer, who gave her some corn for Hen, who gave her some eggs for Shoemaker, and Shoemaker gave her some thread and a sharp, shiny needle.

And Mouse ran happily back home and mended Hedgehog's waistcoat.

THE
FROG PRINCE

Once upon a time, long ago, there was a beautiful princess who lived in a splendid palace. Her father, the king, had given her a golden ball for her birthday and she would spend hours playing with it in the palace gardens, throwing it up into the air and catching it.

One day, she was sitting by a well playing with her golden ball as usual, when the ball bounced out of her hands. Splish, splash! It fell into the well.

"Oh dear! My ball has sunk to the bottom. Whatever shall I do?" said the princess, and she began to cry. Then she heard a noise and, looking down, she saw a frog in the water.

"Don't cry, lovely princess," it croaked. "I can help you."

"How can a frog help me?" wept the princess.

"If I dive into the water and bring up your ball, will you promise to let me eat from your golden plate, sleep in your bed and will you give me a goodnight kiss?"

"I'll promise anything if you manage to find my ball," said the princess. But when the frog dived down under the water, she whispered, "What a silly frog! He can't possibly eat and sleep in the palace."

In a moment, the frog reappeared with the golden ball. The princess was overjoyed, but she had already forgotten about her promise. She only just remembered to say thank you before she snatched the ball away and ran to the palace for dinner.

That evening, as the king, the princess and all the lords and ladies sat eating, they heard a noise at the door. Then a croaky voice called, "Princess, let me in."

The princess ran to open the door and, hippety-hop, the frog jumped into the room. The princess was very cross.

"What is the meaning of this?" demanded the king.

"Oh dear," said the princess, "I made this silly frog a promise today."

"Well, Daughter, promises must be kept," said the king. "Tell me exactly what you promised."

"I promised it could eat from my plate," she said sulkily.

Then the king ordered a servant to put a silk cloth on the table so that the frog could sit by the princess's plate. The frog enjoyed its dinner, but the princess barely touched her food.

That night, when the princess was in bed, the frog hopped into her room.

"Oh," she said with a shudder, "I suppose I must keep my promise to let you sleep on the end of my bed."

She picked the frog up and shivered as she remembered her last promise.

"Must I really give you a goodnight kiss?" she asked.

"Yes, please," croaked the frog.

"I'll get it over with quickly," thought the princess, but when her lips touched the clammy frog, lo and behold, it turned into a handsome prince.

"Thank you," he said, smiling. "You have broken the spell. A cruel witch turned me into a frog. I could only regain my human form if a princess let me eat from her plate, sleep in her bed and then kissed me."

The princess laughed happily.

"Let's tell my father," she said, and they ran downstairs.

Of course, the king was delighted. Before long, the prince and princess fell in love and they had a wonderful wedding. They lived happily ever after, but, every so often, the princess would tease her husband and call him her 'frog prince'.

FIVE
IN A POD

Five green peas grew in a fine green pod. The pod grew. The peas grew.

"What will happen to us, now that we are getting so big?" the peas wondered. The pod turned yellow, and so did the peas. Suddenly the pod was pulled off the pea plant. "How exciting," said the smallest pea. "I wonder where we're going?"

Pop! The pod burst open and the five peas rolled into a little boy's hand.

"These are just the right size for my pop-gun," the boy said. And he loaded the first pea and shot it into the air.

"Whee! I'm flying," called the pea.

"I'm flying to the sun," shouted the second pea when it shot out of the pop-gun.

"We're too tired to fly," grumbled the third and fourth peas, but the little boy shot them high into the air all the same.

"This is exciting," laughed the smallest pea as it sailed into the air. "I wonder where I am flying to?"

The smallest pea landed on the sill of a small window just under the roof of a house. It rolled into a crack filled with soft green moss where it rested very comfortably indeed.

17

In the attic room behind the window lived a poor woman and her daughter. The woman worked hard all day, scrubbing floors, cleaning fireplaces and washing clothes to earn money. She spent all her money on her little daughter, who had been ill for a whole year and had to stay in bed all day while her mother went out to work.

One spring morning, when the little girl awoke, the sun was shining brightly. The girl looked out of the window.

"Whatever is that green thing out there?" she said. "Look, Mama. It's dancing in the wind."

Her mother opened the window wide.

"My goodness!" she exclaimed. "It's a little pea plant. However did it get up here?" She pushed her daughter's bed nearer the window. "Look! It can be your special garden."

That night, when her mother came home, the little girl said, "The pea plant looks happy. It likes the sunshine. It's made me feel better already!"

The mother was delighted. She tied a little stick to the plant so that the wind couldn't break it. Then she stretched a piece of string across the window for the pea plant to twist round and climb.

"Mama!" cried the little girl one morning. "Come and look! My plant has grown some pretty pink and white flowers." Delighted, she struggled to sit up.

In a day or two she was strong enough to leave her bed. Then she sat happily in the sunshine by the window, looking after her tiny garden with its single plant.

But what had happened to the other four peas? A blackbird had gobbled up the first one. The two lazy peas had been eaten by a pigeon, and the one that had wanted to fly to the sun had fallen into a pond, where it had swelled and swelled until it almost burst.

As the little girl grew strong and well, her eyes sparkled again. And the flowers on her pea plant soon turned into fat, green pods, filled with fat, green peas.

THE DAY
THE SKY FELL DOWN

In a field on a farm there grew a big chestnut tree. One day, a chicken called Chicky-Licky was sleeping under this tree when suddenly a prickly chestnut fell, plop, onto her head.

"Oh my, the sky is falling down!" she exclaimed. "I'd better run and tell everyone about it." So she ran and ran until she met a speckledy hen.

"Henny-Penny," cried Chicky-Licky, quite out of breath, "the sky is falling down. A piece fell on me."

"We must tell the king about this," said Henny-Penny. So off they ran until they met Ducky-Lucky.

"Ducky-Lucky," clucked Henny-Penny, "the sky is falling down. A piece just fell on Chicky-Licky and we're going to tell the king about it."

"I'll come with you," quacked Ducky-Lucky. So the three birds ran and ran until they met Goosey-Loosey.

"Goosey-Loosey," clucked Henny-Penny, "the sky is falling down. A big piece fell on Chicky-Licky and we're off to tell the king."

"I'm coming too," screeched Goosey-Loosey. So the four birds ran and ran until they met Turkey-Lurkey.

20

"Turkey-Lurkey," cried Henny-Penny, "have you heard the news? The sky is falling down and a great big piece fell on Chicky-Licky. We're on our way to tell the king all about it."

"I'm coming too," gobbled Turkey-Lurkey. So the five birds ran and ran until they met Foxy-Loxy.

"Foxy-Loxy," clucked Henny-Penny, "the sky is falling down. An enormous piece fell on Chicky-Licky and we are on our way to tell the king about it."

"Well, well, well," said Foxy-Loxy. "His Majesty will be most interested. Do you know where he lives?"

"Certainly," replied Henny-Penny. "He lives in a castle with a golden roof and diamonds in the windows."

"I'm afraid you are wrong, Henny-Penny," said Foxy-Loxy. "He lives in a palace under the hill. His Majesty often asks me to visit him, so I know the way very well."

"Please could you show us the way then?" cried the five birds together, flapping their wings excitedly.

"It will be a pleasure," grinned Foxy-Loxy, trying to hide his large teeth under his ginger whiskers. "It isn't very far from here at all. Just keep close behind me and I will lead you straight there!"

So the five birds and Foxy-Loxy ran and ran until they came to a deep hole in the hillside.

"Keep close to me," called Foxy-Loxy. So Chicky-Licky and Henny-Penny and Ducky-Lucky and Goosey-Loosey and Turkey-Lurkey all followed Foxy-Loxy closely down the hole and into the hillside.

Of course, Foxy-Loxy had led them right into his den and, sad to say, not one of those birds came out again.

THE CLEVER LITTLE GIRL
AND THE BEAR

One day, a little girl called Joanna set off with her friends to pick berries in the woods. They had not gone far when Joanna spotted a bush covered with juicy berries, so she stopped to fill her basket. Joanna was so busy picking that she forgot all about the time and her friends until she suddenly noticed that it was getting dark. She called out to her friends, but there was no reply. She wandered this way and that, but she couldn't find them, and she was soon lost.

Then, through the trees, she saw a cottage.

"Somebody there will show me the way home," she thought. She went up to the cottage and knocked on the door. Nobody answered, so she pushed the door open and peeped inside. It looked so warm and cosy that she tiptoed in and sat down by the fire.

Presently, a huge bear walked in.

"Who are you, little girl?" he roared. "And what are you doing in my house?"

"My name is Joanna," whispered the terrified little girl.

"Well, now that you are here," growled the bear, "you can keep my house clean and tidy, and cook my supper every day.

And don't try to run away, for I would soon catch you and gobble you up."

"I'd better do what the bear says," Joanna thought. So she cooked and cleaned for the bear, but all the time she was thinking of a way to escape.

At last she had a wonderful idea. One night, when the bear had finished his supper, Joanna said sweetly, "Bear, please will you take a present to my dear parents for me?"

"Certainly," grunted the bear.

So Joanna baked lots of apple pies and packed them in a large, bear-sized basket.

"You must not eat any of the pies," she said. "I will know at once if you do."

"Of course I won't," replied the bear. Then he left the kitchen to fetch his walking stick and, quick as a flash, Joanna crept inside the basket and hid under the apple pies.

When the bear returned, he heaved the basket onto his back and lumbered away. He had not gone far when he said, "These pies smell good. I think I'll take a rest and nibble one."

But as he took out a pie, he heard Joanna's voice.

"You're eating my pies," she said.

Up jumped the bear.

"Oh dear, what sharp eyes that girl has," he grunted, and he walked on.

"She can't see me now," he thought after a time, and so he took another pie out of the basket. But before he could take a bite, he heard Joanna's voice.

"Caught you again, Bear, haven't I?" she said.

"She can see me through the trees!" he exclaimed. "She must have magic eyes." And he dashed to the village and knocked on Joanna's parents' door. Just then, three dogs appeared, barking and snapping at the bear's heels. The bear was so frightened that he dropped the basket and ran back to the woods as fast as he could.

When Joanna's mother and father opened the door, Joanna jumped out of the basket. Her mother and father were delighted to see their daughter safe and sound and they all lived happily ever after.

ELEPHANT BIG
AND
ELEPHANT LITTLE

Elephant Big was always boasting.

"I'm bigger and better than you," he told Elephant Little. "I can run faster, and shoot water higher out of my trunk, and eat more, and…"

"No. You can't!" said Elephant Little.

Elephant Big was surprised. Elephant Big was *always* right. Then he curled up his trunk and laughed and laughed.

"What's more, I'll show you," said Elephant Little. "Let's have a running race, and a shooting-water-out-of-our-trunks race, and an eating race. We'll soon see who wins."

"I shall, of course," boasted Elephant Big. "Lion shall be judge."

"The running race first!" Lion said. "Run two miles there and two miles back. One of you runs in the field, the other one runs in the forest. Elephant Big shall choose."

Elephant Big thought and thought, and Elephant Little pretended to talk to himself: "I hope he chooses to run in the field, because *I* want to run in the forest."

When Elephant Big heard this, he thought: "If Elephant Little wants very much to run in the forest, that means the forest is best." Aloud he said: "I choose the forest."

"Very well," said Lion. "One, two, three. Go!"

Elephant Little had short legs, but they ran very fast on the springy smooth grass of the field. Elephant Big had long, strong legs, but they could not carry him quickly along through the forest. Broken branches lay in his way; thorns tore at him; tangled grass caught at his feet. By the time he stumbled, tired and panting, back to the winning post, Elephant Little had run his four miles, and was standing talking to Lion.

"What ages you've been!" said Elephant Little. "We thought you were lost."

"Elephant Little wins," said Lion.

Elephant Little smiled to himself.

"But I'll win the next race," said Elephant Big. "I can shoot water much higher than you can."

"All right!" said Lion. "One of you fills his trunk from the river, the other fills his trunk from the lake. Elephant Big shall choose."

Elephant Big thought and thought, and Elephant Little pretended to talk to himself: "I hope he chooses the river, because *I* want to fill my trunk from the lake."

When Elephant Big heard this, he thought: "If Elephant Little wants very much to fill his trunk from the lake, that means the lake is best." Aloud he said: "I choose the lake."

"Very well!" said Lion. "One, two, three. Go!"

Elephant Little ran to the river and filled his trunk with clear, sparkling water. His trunk was small, but he spouted the water as high as a tree.

Elephant Big ran to the lake, and filled his long, strong trunk with water. But the lake water was heavy with mud, and full of slippery, tickly fishes. When Elephant Big spouted it out, it rose only as high as a middle-sized thorn bush. He lifted his trunk and tried harder than ever. A cold little fish slipped down his throat, and Elephant Big spluttered and choked.

"Elephant Little wins," said Lion.

Elephant Little smiled to himself.

When Elephant Big stopped coughing, he said: "But I'll win the next race, see if I don't. I can eat much more than you can."

"Very well!" said Lion. "Eat where you like and how you like."

Elephant Big thought and thought, and Elephant Little pretended to talk to himself: "I must eat and eat as fast as I can, and I mustn't stop; not for a minute."

Elephant Big thought to himself: "Then I must do exactly the same. I must eat and eat as fast as I can, and I mustn't stop;

28

not for a minute."

"Are you ready?" asked Lion. "One, two, three. Go!"

Elephant Big bit and swallowed, and bit and swallowed, as fast as he could, without stopping. Before very long, he began to feel full up inside.

Elephant Little bit and swallowed, and bit and swallowed. Then he stopped eating and ran round a thorn bush three times. He felt perfectly well inside.

Elephant Big went on biting and swallowing, biting and swallowing, without stopping. He began to feel very, very funny inside.

Elephant Little bit and swallowed, and bit and swallowed. Then again he stopped eating, and ran round a thorn bush six times. He felt perfectly well inside.

Elephant Big bit and swallowed, and bit and swallowed, as fast as he could, without stopping once, until he felt so dreadfully ill inside that he had to sit down.

Elephant Little had just finished running around a thorn bush nine times, and he still felt perfectly well inside. When he saw Elephant Big on the ground, holding his tummy and groaning horribly, Elephant Little smiled to himself.

"Oh, I do like eating, don't you?" he said. "I've only just started. I could eat and eat and eat and eat."

"Oh, oh, oh!" groaned Elephant Big.

"Why, what's the matter?" asked Elephant Little. "You look queer. Sort of green! When are you going to start eating again?"

"Not a single leaf more!" groaned Elephant Big. "Not a blade of grass, not a twig can I eat!"

"Elephant Little wins," said Lion.

Elephant Big felt too ill to speak.

After that day, if Elephant Big began to boast, Elephant Little smiled, and said: "Shall we have a running race? Shall we spout water? Or shall we just eat and eat and eat?"

Then Elephant Big would remember. Before very long, he was one of the nicest, most friendly elephants ever to take a mud bath.

WHY THE RAVEN HAS BLACK FEATHERS

Long ago, the raven was a handsome bird with snow-white feathers and magic powers. One day, he saw some people chewing tree roots and digging in the dusty earth for food.

"I must help them," he thought, and he flew down to them calling, "Caw! Caw! Caw!"

The people saw him and shouted, "Here is Put-it-Right-Raven! Perhaps he will help us find some food."

The raven picked up a few dry leaves and scattered them on a small pond. Immediately, the water began to hubble and bubble, the leaves vanished and dozens of fishes jumped in the water, their silvery sides gleaming in the sun.

The people were thrilled. They had a good meal of fishes, but when they had finished, they realized that their pond had dried up. So they asked Put-it-Right-Raven to help them again.

The raven could find only one well in the whole world. It was in the house of a man called Ganook, but Ganook would not give any of his water away.

The raven thought he might be able to drink enough water to carry back to his friends. He flew to Ganook's house and begged Ganook for a drink of water.

"I can spare only three sips," said Ganook, "so don't drink any more than that." And he showed the raven his well.

The raven sipped, and then tried to gulp. But he began to wobble and Ganook saw him.

"Stop that, Raven," he cried. "Do you want to drink my well dry?"

That was exactly what the raven wanted to do. But instead he said, "Ganook, I shall tell you a story." So they settled down comfortably and the raven began: "It was a dark and stormy night when the chief said to his storyteller, 'Storyteller, tell me a story.' So the storyteller began: 'It was a dark and stormy night when the chief said to his storyteller, 'Storyteller, tell me a story.' So the storyteller began…"

The raven's voice was slow and gentle. Over and over again he started the story until Ganook began to doze. As soon as Ganook's eyes were closed, the raven dashed to the well and started to drink, but Ganook was not quite asleep.

"Get on with the story," he said. "I'm not asleep." Then he opened one eye and cried, "Where are you, Raven?"

"Just stretching my legs," the raven answered, and his voice droned on and on: "It was a dull and dreary night when the chief said to his storyteller, 'Snore, snore, snore'," and that is just what Ganook finally did!

Quietly, the raven went to the well again. Glub, slurp, gulp! He drank every last drop of water, but as he closed his beak, Ganook woke up.

"You've tricked me!" yelled Ganook. "I'll teach you to steal my water." And he seized a stick to beat the raven. Flapping his wings, the raven flew up the chimney. But he was so full of water that he got stuck. Ganook stoked up the fire so that smoke rose up the chimney. The smoke made the poor raven choke and turned his snow-white feathers quite black. He struggled and struggled until at last he heaved himself out of the top of the chimney. Then he flew off, barely able to keep above the trees of the forest he was so weighed down by the water.

As the raven flew, drops of water fell from his beak and made rivers and lakes of fresh, cool water on the Earth. Thanks to the raven's courage, the people never lacked water again. But ever since then, his feathers have been as black as soot.

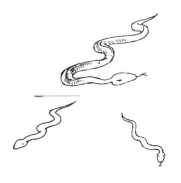

SAINT PATRICK AND THE SNAKES

Long, long ago, a good and holy man called Patrick visited Ireland. There the people told him all about the trouble they had with snakes. There were thousands of them! They ate the farmers' corn, chickens and even their potatoes.

Now, whenever Patrick walked by, the snakes would slither out of his way and slip into the beautiful Irish lakes to hide. But they would still slide out again sometimes, when Patrick wasn't there, and scare everybody.

One day, Patrick, who had been made a saint soon after his arrival in Ireland, said to himself, "There are not as many snakes in Ireland now, but there are still enough to scare

everyone. If their numbers start to increase again, then what will happen to the poor people? I'd better see what I can do."

Saint Patrick wandered along by a huge lake near a place called Kerry, thinking about how to get rid of the snakes. As he was walking, a farmer rushed out to meet him.

"Are you Saint Patrick?" he cried. "If you are, please help me. The largest snake I've ever seen is swallowing my sheep! There is nothing I can do to make it go away."

"There now," said Saint Patrick calmly, "of course I'll help you, don't worry."

He went alone to the lakeside and said a prayer. Then he called out, "Monster Snake, come out of the water! Go to the sea and leave Ireland forever."

But the snake did not obey him.

"So," said Saint Patrick, "the snake thinks it is safe if it stays under water. Well then, I'll change the water. I will get rid of all the snakes in Ireland by simply changing the water in every single lake!"

That night, Saint Patrick warned everybody to lock up their animals.

"Stay inside with your children and don't be scared, no matter what happens," he said. Then he went back to the lake.

The snake saw him saying his prayers and hissed to itself, "I'm perfectly safe if I stay in the lake." But it found that the clear, cool lake water was changing. The water started to get warmer and warmer. Soon it was very hot and then it was boiling hot. The long snake lifted its head above the water and thrashed its tail, spurting water everywhere. But good Saint Patrick did not move. At last the snake could bear it no longer. It raced across the lake and climbed out. Then it slithered over the fields, not even stopping to eat. All it wanted was to reach the sea and to cool down in the water, as far away from Saint Patrick as possible.

That same night, there were horrible hissings and screechings all over Ireland as snakes rushed to the sea. Saint Patrick stayed at the lakeside until sunrise, when the last sizzling snake had slithered under the waves.

"Saint Patrick has rid Ireland of all its snakes," the people cried. "And our lakes are fresh and sparkling again."

What is more, to this very day, not a single snake is to be found anywhere in Ireland.

THE HAZELNUT CHILD

Once upon a time, there lived a man and his wife. They had no children, but they wished every day that they might have one, even if it were no bigger than a hazelnut.

At last their wish was answered and they had a baby boy. But the baby was, indeed, no bigger than a hazelnut, and he never grew any bigger.

One day, when the hazelnut child was fifteen years old, he was sitting on the table beside his mother. She turned to him and said, "You are fifteen years old now and must learn to look after yourself. How are you going to earn your living?"

"I'll be a messenger," answered the hazelnut child.

His mother burst out laughing.

"What an idea!" she said. "You a messenger! Why, your little feet would take an hour to go the distance an ordinary person could walk in a minute."

But the hazelnut child replied, "All the same, I am going to be a messenger. Just give me something to do and you'll see. I shall be back in next to no time."

So his mother said, "Very well. Go to your aunt in the next village and fetch me a comb."

The hazelnut child jumped up immediately and ran out into the street. There he found a man on horseback who was just setting out for the next village. He crept up the horse's leg, sat down under the saddle and began to pinch the horse. The horse reared up in surprise and set off at a gallop with its rider clinging on for dear life.

When they reached the next village, the hazelnut child stopped pinching the horse, which was now so tired that it could only walk very slowly, and slipped down its leg to the ground. He ran to his aunt and asked for the comb. Then he made the return journey in the same way as before.

His mother was amazed when the hazelnut child walked through the door.

"How did you manage to be so quick?" she asked when he handed her the comb.

The hazelnut child just smiled and said, "Ah, Mother, now you see I was right when I said that I would earn my living as a messenger."

When he was twenty years old, the hazelnut child said to his parents, "Farewell, my dear mother and father. I am going out into the world. When I am rich, I will return to you."

His father and mother laughed at the little man's words and did not believe him for a moment.

That night, the hazelnut child crept out onto the roof, where some storks had built their nests. The storks were fast asleep, so he climbed onto the back of one of them and fastened a silk cord round one of its wings. Then he crept among its soft, downy feathers and fell asleep.

The next morning, the stork flew off towards the south, for winter was coming. And the hazelnut child flew with them, holding on to the silk cord.

Over the land and over the sea and over the great desert they flew, until they came at last to a warm land in the south. Here the storks set up their nests in a great city.

The hazelnut child climbed down off the stork. When the people saw him, they were astonished and took him straight to their king.

The king was delighted with the tiny man and asked him to stay with him. So the hazelnut child lived with the king and became his friend.

Then, one day, the hazelnut child said to the king, "I left my mother and father far away in my own country. I miss them and wish to return to them."

The king was sad to lose his little friend, but he understood. As a parting gift, he gave the hazelnut child a great diamond four times as large as himself.

The hazelnut child went back to the storks, who were about to fly north once again. He fastened his diamond firmly under the neck of one with a ribbon. Then he tied on a silk cord as before and climbed onto the stork's back.

Over the great desert, over the sea and over the land they flew, until they reached the chimney of the house of the hazelnut child.

When the storks were settled in their nests, the hazelnut child took his diamond, climbed down into his house and ran to his parents. They cried with joy at his safe return and stared in astonishment at the diamond. They sold it the very next day and got enough money to live happily for the rest of their lives.

THE
BIG TURNIP

A little old man, a little old woman, a little girl, a little black cat and a little grey mouse lived happily together in a little house with a little garden.

One day, the little old man said to his wife, "I'm going into the garden to plant a turnip seed." So he went outside, dug a hole and dropped in a turnip seed.

"I must water it well," he said to himself, "then it will grow into a fine turnip."

Soon the seed began to grow. It grew until it was as big as the old man's head. It grew some more until it was as big as the old man's head and the old woman's head put together. When it had grown twice as big as both their heads, the old man said to his wife, "Today I will pull up the turnip. Then we can have boiled turnip for dinner!"

41

The little old woman found a large pan. She filled it with water and put it on the fire. Her husband went into the garden to dig up his turnip. He took hold of its leaves and pulled. But he couldn't pull the turnip up.

"Wife, Wife," he shouted, "come and help me to pull up the turnip."

So his wife held him round his middle and together they pulled and pulled, but they could not pull up the turnip.

Then the little old woman called out, "Little Girl, please come and help us to pull up this turnip."

So the little girl grabbed hold of the little old woman and the little old woman took hold of her husband and together they pulled and they pulled, but the turnip still did not budge.

"Little Black Cat," called the little girl, "come and help us to pull up the turnip."

The black cat jumped off the windowsill. He took hold of the little girl, who took hold of the little old woman, who took hold of the little old man. They pulled and they pulled, but it was no use, they could not pull up the turnip.

42

Then the little black cat called out, "Little Grey Mouse, come and help us to pull up the turnip."

The little grey mouse came running out of the house. He took hold of the little black cat, who took hold of the little girl, who took hold of the little old woman, who took hold of the little old man. They pulled and they pulled until UP! came the turnip at last. They were pulling so hard that the little old man fell back on top of his wife, who fell on top of the little girl, who fell on top of the little black cat, who fell on top of the little grey mouse!

When they had all got up and dusted themselves down, they rolled the turnip into the house. They chopped it up and put it into the pot on the fire. Then they all had boiled turnip for dinner!

BILLY BEAR'S
STUMPY TAIL

One wintry day, Billy Bear met Folly Fox slinking round a frozen pond. Folly Fox was trying to hide a net full of fishes that he had just stolen.

"Where did you get such fine fishes?" demanded Billy Bear.

"I caught them, of course," replied Folly quickly.

"I would really like to catch some fishes," said Billy. "How did you do it?"

Now Folly Fox was jealous of Billy Bear's beautiful bushy tail, so he laughed and said, "It's easy, old friend. You slide onto the ice and cut a hole. Then you dangle your lovely bushy tail down, down into the water, sit on the ice and wait for the fishes to nibble."

Billy Bear wrinkled his nose and pulled a long face.

"Isn't there another way to catch fishes?" he growled.

"Not if you want such fine ones as these," said Folly Fox. "Anyway, it's easy. All you have to remember, dear friend, is to keep your tail in the hole. If you feel a few little nibbles or some pinches now and then, don't take any notice. Just remember that the fishes are biting and hanging on to your long tail and that, the longer you wait, the more fishes you'll catch!"

Billy Bear growled and grunted suspiciously.

"How do I get the fishes out of the water then?" he asked.

"That's easy for a strong bear," chuckled Folly. "First you give a great big push onto your right side then you push yourself over to your left side. Then you stand up quickly and start counting your fishes."

Billy Bear was now convinced.

"My tail is much bigger than yours," he boasted, "so I'm sure to catch twice as many fishes as you did."

He lumbered onto the ice, cut out a hole and sat down. Then he wiggled and waggled until his tail was dangling in the

45

water. My, it was cold! But Billy thought about the wonderful dinner he would soon be having and pushed his tail down deeper into the hole.

Soon his tail was frozen fast in the pond and Billy was shivering with cold.

"Time to go," he chuckled in his growly voice. He rolled over onto his right side. Nothing moved. He pushed hard onto his left side. There was a little creak, creak. Then he heaved himself up with all his strength, just as Folly Fox had told him to. CRACK! His tail snapped right off.

Sadly, Billy Bear crawled off the ice. He hadn't caught a single fish and he'd lost his beautiful tail. It never did grow again and that is why, to this day, all bears have stumpy tails.

THE
THREE BROTHERS

There was once a man who had three sons. His only possession was his house and, as he loved each of his sons just as much as the others, he could not decide which of them should have his house when he died.

At last he had an idea. He said to his sons, "You must all go and learn a trade. When you return, whoever can show that he is the most skilled at his trade shall have the house."

The sons all agreed to this plan. The eldest wanted to be a blacksmith, the second a barber and the third a fencing-master, teaching people to fight with swords. Bidding their father farewell, the three brothers set off to learn their chosen trades. They worked hard and soon became experts.

The blacksmith got a job shoeing the king's horses. He thought to himself, "I am the most skilled blacksmith in the land, the house will be mine, without a doubt!"

The barber shaved the most important men in the kingdom and he too was sure the house would be his.

The fencing-master had to work very hard and was often hit by the swords during fencing matches, but people were soon flocking to see his wonderful sword play.

47

At last it was time to return home. The brothers went back to their father's house and they all sat down to decide how each could show off his skill.

As they were talking, they saw a hare running across the field towards them.

"Look!" said the barber. "Here is my chance." He seized a basin and soap and his sharpest razor. Then, as the hare ran past him, the barber shaved its whiskers without cutting or hurting another hair on its body.

"I like that very much indeed," said his father. "Unless your brothers can do better, this house shall be yours."

Soon afterwards, they saw a man driving a carriage down the road at great speed.

"Now, Father, you shall see what I can do," said the blacksmith. He rushed after the carriage, took off the horse's four shoes and shod it with four new ones without the horse even slowing down.

48

"You are a clever fellow!" said the father. "You know your trade just as well as your brother. I really don't know which of you should have the house."

The third son said, "You have not seen what I can do yet."

Just then it started to rain. The third brother rushed outside, drew his sword and swung it fast in cross cuts above his head. He swung it so fast that it stopped any drops of rain from falling on him. Heavier and heavier fell the rain, but the young man just swung his sword faster and faster, and he kept as dry as if he were under a roof.

The father was delighted when he saw this and said, "You, my son, have the most skill, so you shall have the house."

The other two brothers agreed with their father and praised their brother too.

After that, the three brothers stayed with their father, each plying his own trade. When at last the father died, the youngest brother did not take the house for himself. Instead, he shared it with his brothers, and they all lived together until the end of their days.

THE CAT
AND
THE MOUSE

A cat and a mouse became friends and decided to share a house together.

One day, the cat said, "We must get food for the winter or we shall go hungry." So they bought a little pot of fat and hid it in the church.

"Nobody will expect to find a pot of fat in the church, so it will be quite safe," said the cat. "We can leave it there and not touch it until we need to."

But the cat could not stop thinking about the little pot of fat and of how good it would taste. Finally she could wait no longer, so she went to the mouse and said, "My cousin has had a dear little kitten and she wants me to be its godmother. Do you mind if I go out today to visit her?"

"Of course you must go," said the kind mouse.

Now the cat had not really been asked to be a godmother, and she did not go to visit her cousin. Instead, she slunk off to the church, took the little pot of fat out of its hiding place and licked the top off. Then she went for a walk on the rooftops of the town and returned home.

"Did you have a nice time?" asked the mouse. "What is the kitten's name?"

"Top Off," said the cat, which was the first thing that came into her head.

"Top Off?" echoed the mouse. "What a strange name!"

Soon the cat longed for another taste of fat. So she went to the mouse and said, "I have been asked to be a godmother for a second time and I promised that I would go and visit the dear little kitten today."

Again the mouse agreed, and again the cat sneaked off to the church. This time she ate half the pot of fat. When she came home, the mouse asked, "What is this kitten called?"

"Half Gone," answered the cat, licking her lips.

"Half Gone? What a name!" said the surprised mouse.

Before long, the cat's mouth began to water once again at the thought of the pot of fat.

"All good things come in threes," she told the mouse. "I again have to be a godmother and must go and see the kitten."

The cat frisked off to the church, where she ate up every bit of fat. When she got home, the mouse asked at once about the third kitten's name.

"It won't please you any better," said the cat. "He is called All Gone."

"All Gone!" repeated the mouse. "All Gone! What can it mean?" But she did not guess.

When winter came and there was no food outside, the mouse remembered their winter store. She said to the cat, "Come, Cat. We'll go and fetch our pot of fat. I'm sure it will taste very good."

The cat said nothing, but she went with the mouse to the church. There was the little pot, but it was quite, quite empty.

"Ah!" cried the mouse. "Now I see what has happened. You are no true friend of mine! You ate all the fat when you pretended to be a godmother – first you licked the *top off*, then you licked until it was *half gone*, then..."

But the cat did not wait to hear the end. She rushed out of the church and the mouse never saw her again.

Goldilocks
and
The Three Bears

Once upon a time, there was a great big father bear, a middle-sized mother bear and a tiny baby bear. They lived in a house in the forest. One morning, they made some porridge for breakfast and poured it into three bowls. As it was too hot to eat, they decided to go for an early morning walk.

While they were out, a little girl called Goldilocks came walking up to their house. She knocked on the door, but when nobody answered, she pushed it open and went inside.

In front of her there was a table with a great big chair, a middle-sized chair and a tiny chair. On the table she saw one great big bowl and spoon, one middle-sized bowl and spoon and one tiny bowl and spoon.

Goldilocks was hungry after her walk, so she sat in the great big chair, picked up the great big spoon and tasted the porridge in the great big bowl. But the chair was so hard and the porridge was so hot that she jumped down quickly. Next she tried the middle-sized chair and the middle-sized bowl of porridge. But this chair was too soft and the porridge was too sweet. Finally Goldilocks sat down in the tiny chair. She picked up the tiny spoon and tried some porridge from the tiny bowl.

The porridge was neither too hot nor too sweet, it was just right. In fact, it was so good that she ate it all up. When she had finished, Goldilocks settled back in the tiny chair, but she was too heavy for it and it broke into little pieces.

Goldilocks felt very sleepy after her breakfast, so she went upstairs. There she found a great big bed, a middle-sized bed and a tiny bed. She climbed onto the great big bed, but it was too hard. She lay on the middle-sized bed, but it was so soft that she sank right down into it. Then she tried the tiny bed. It felt snug and warm and Goldilocks fell fast asleep.

While Goldilocks was sleeping, the three bears came home, feeling hungry. But when they went to sit down and eat their porridge, something was definitely not right.

Father Bear looked at his chair and growled in his great big voice, "Somebody has been sitting in my chair."

Then Mother Bear said in her middle-sized voice, "Somebody has been sitting in my chair."

When Baby Bear saw his chair in pieces all over the floor, he squeaked in his tiny voice, "Somebody has been sitting in my chair and broken it."

Then Father Bear saw his spoon sticking out of his bowl.

"Somebody has been eating my porridge," he growled in his great big voice.

Mother Bear saw the spoon in her bowl.

"Somebody has been eating my porridge," she said in her middle-sized voice.

Baby Bear looked inside his bowl and squeaked, "Somebody has been eating my porridge and has eaten it all up!"

The bears stomped upstairs. Father Bear saw the rumpled bedclothes on his bed and growled in his great big voice, "Somebody has been sleeping in my bed."

Mother Bear saw that her pillow was not straight.

"Somebody has been sleeping in my bed," she said in her middle-sized voice.

Then Baby Bear looked at his bed.

"Somebody is sleeping in my bed NOW," he squeaked.

Baby Bear's sharp squeak woke Goldilocks. She saw the three bears standing round her and got such a fright she fell out of bed. Picking herself up, she ran from the house as fast as she could, and the three bears never saw her again.

HOW THE CRAB GOT ITS HARD BACK

Once upon a time, there were two sisters called Avallonia and Grafina who lived together in a little house near a river. The two sisters were not a bit alike. Avallonia was not pretty, but she was kind and gentle and would sing merrily as she cleaned and polished their little house. Her older sister, Grafina, was lazy and horrid to everyone she met. She was, however, very beautiful and laughed unkindly at her sister Avallonia.

One morning, as Avallonia walked to the river to get some water, she met an old, sick woman. The woman was trying to wash her bare back. When she saw the girl, she whispered feebly, "Will you scratch and wash my back? Wash and scratch and scrub really hard, mind!"

Avallonia noticed that the old woman's back was hard and rough. It felt like broken glass, but she felt sorry for the woman and so she washed and scratched, scratched and washed until her hands began to bleed.

At last the old woman said sweetly, "Thank you, my dear. You have been very kind to me. I'd like to give you a special present. What would you like best of all?"

The woman looked so thin and ill that Avallonia did not like to ask for anything.

"Your thanks will do for me," she replied.

"Then thank you again," the old woman said. "But look in the river before you go."

The girl bent over the water and, to her surprise, she saw that she now had the most beautiful face you could imagine. When she looked up again, the old woman had vanished.

Avallonia was now lovelier than her sister and Grafina was furious when she heard her story.

"What a stupid sister I have," she thought. "I would have asked for lots of money. Then I'd buy a wonderful house and I'd never have to do any more cleaning."

With this in mind, she rushed off to the river to find the old woman. When she got there, she saw the ugliest woman in the world sitting on the bank. Her bare back was cracked and scaly, and her hands and feet were bent like thin, sharp claws.

When she saw Grafina, the old woman screeched, "Wash and scratch. Scratch and wash my back."

But Grafina could not bring herself to touch the ugly old woman's back.

"Get out of my way, you horrible ugly wretch," she shouted. "Scratch your back yourself – your claws look sharp enough." And she gave the old woman a hard push.

"What a rude girl you are," the woman said. "I may look ugly to you, but now you look ugly to me."

No sooner had the old woman finished speaking than Grafina's beauty vanished and she felt herself shrinking and shrivelling. Her hands and feet changed into claws and her back turned into a hard, crinkly shell.

Now she hides in the mud or in the sand and, when her back itches, she lets the river wash over her, for no one will scratch her back. After all, who wants to scratch a crab?

THE MONTHS
OF THE YEAR

Once upon a time, in Italy, there were two brothers. Geroni was very rich, but he was mean, and he would not lend his poorer brother Emilio a single penny.

One cold day in March, Emilio went off to find work. He searched all day until at last he came to an inn. When he went inside, he found twelve men sitting round a fire.

"There's room over here," one of them called, and Emilio was pleased to sit by the fire and get warm. Everybody started chatting. One of the men, who had a fierce face and a loud voice, turned to Emilio.

"What do you think about this terrible weather, eh? March is such a cold month, don't you think?" he said.

"I don't mind it," replied Emilio thoughtfully. "Each month of the year has a special job to do. In winter we say it's too cold. In summer we grumble that it's too hot. But if it never rained, the seeds wouldn't grow, and if the sun didn't shine, we'd never get any fruit or flowers. I think we need all the different months."

"Well spoken," said the man. "But the month of March is horrible. The snow, fogs and frost make us all miserable."

"Ah, those are the bad things," said Emilio. "But look at the buds on the trees! You know that spring is coming when March is here."

The fierce-looking man was delighted.

"I am March," he told Emilio, "and these are my eleven brothers, January to December. Thank you for your kind words. Please take this box and, whenever you need anything, just open it."

Emilio slept well that night and the next day he set off home. The snow was deep and soon Emilio was freezing cold. He decided to test the box. Opening the lid, he said, "I wish I had a carriage to ride in."

Instantly a carriage and horses appeared. Emilio was soon warm and snug inside the coach, but then he began to feel hungry. He opened the box again and wished for his favourite food. The words were hardly out of his mouth before a delicious meal appeared, and Emilio ate until he could eat no more. Later on, he wished for clothes fit for a prince. As he put on a wonderful velvet cloak, he chuckled to himself, "Whatever will my brother say?"

Geroni was very envious when his brother arrived home.

"How did you manage to get these magnificent things?" he spluttered.

Emilio told him about the twelve brothers at the inn and the wonderful gift, but he did not say who the men were!

Geroni set off immediately. He found the inn and saw the twelve men by the fire. Pushing one of them aside so that he could sit by the fire himself, Geroni started to grumble.

"March is a horrible month," he moaned. "The frost kills the seeds and the winds give us colds. It would be a good idea to get rid of March altogether!"

Nobody said a word, but, next morning, March gave Geroni a fine strong stick.

"Whenever you need something, ask this stick to give you a hundred. You will get a big surprise," he said.

Geroni hurried home. He wanted to fill a big room with gold, so he said, "Stick, stick, give me a hundred." Then Geroni got his big surprise. The stick jumped up and beat him fifty, sixty, seventy times!

Luckily, Emilio heard his brother's shouts. He opened his magic box and asked for the stick to stop beating Geroni. When the stick was still, Geroni grumbled about the twelve brothers.

"It's your own fault," Emilio told him. "You were very rude to them. But cheer up, I'll share my box with you. After all, you are my brother."

This made Geroni feel ashamed that he had always been so mean to his brother and he promised to change his ways. And from that day on, Geroni and Emilio shared everything and lived together happily and peacefully.

POLLY
AND THE
BUCKETS OF MILK

Early one misty morning, as the sun was just rising in the sky, Polly, the farmer's daughter, came hurrying through the farmyard with two buckets, each one full to the brim with delicious fresh milk. She was going to sell the milk at the market. Opening the farmyard gate, she slid through quietly, then let the gate swing shut behind her.

Striding off in her smart, red, market-day shoes, Polly began to imagine what she would do when she had sold her two buckets of milk.

"I should get enough money for this milk to buy three hundred brown eggs," she said. "And when the eggs hatch, there will be three hundred chicks to run around my feet!"

Polly cheeped and chirruped as she pretended to be a baby chick pecking at corn in the farmyard. The buckets of milk swayed to and fro as she hurried along the road.

"Now," she thought to herself, "if I feed my fluffy little chicks every day, they should grow into nice plump chickens in time for the Christmas market!"

Polly's eyes grew wider as she thought about selling her three hundred chickens.

"And if I sell every single chicken, I'll have enough money to buy a beautiful blue dress for the Christmas ball. I'll be the prettiest girl there, and I'll dance all night and it will be the most wonderful ball ever!" she said to herself, and with a flick of her skirts, Polly began to swirl and turn, dancing to the sound of the milk as it swished in the buckets.

"What if…" thought Polly suddenly, "what if a young man asks me to marry him at the ball?" She walked more slowly as she imagined what the young man might look like. Then another idea came into her head: "What if not just one, but lots and lots of men ask me to marry them at the ball?" Polly stopped in her tracks as she imagined all the young men crowding round her.

"But, of course," she laughed proudly, "I shall refuse them all!" And with that she tossed her head into the air, tripped over a stone and fell headlong into the hedge.

The milk went everywhere. Splosh! Splash! Splosh! It made puddles all over the path. Polly got soaked, and she shrieked as her buckets and dreams crashed down around her. Polly's eyes filled with tears as she struggled to her feet.

"Now I have no milk to sell at the market!" she sobbed. "And with no milk there will be no money for eggs. With no eggs there will be no chicks, with no chicks there will be no chickens, with no chickens there will be no new dress, and with no new dress there will be no…"

But all this thinking was too much for poor Polly. She wiped away her tears and picked up the empty buckets. The milk puddles glistened like snow in the sunshine. Polly sighed deeply; she had made the mistake of daydreaming and of counting her chickens before they were hatched. There was nothing for her to do now but squelch home in her milky shoes with two empty buckets rattling at her sides.

THE BEST THING TO DO

There was once a flock of goats. The oldest goat could not walk very fast; she was always last when the goats came home from the fields and, one day, she was so slow that she was left behind on the hillside. After wandering around for a little while, the old goat saw a cave.

"The best thing to do is to spend the night in that cave," she thought, so she trotted inside.

But oh, what a fright she got! There was a lion standing inside the cave. He had smelled her. He had seen her. He was ready to attack!

"Help! What shall I do?" thought the goat. "I know! I'll pretend I'm not frightened of his huge head and his pointed teeth. That's the best thing to do."

The lion was astonished when the goat marched up to him, because animals usually ran away from him. They never marched boldly into his cave. He decided not to attack, but he roared, "Who are you? What are you doing here?"

"I'm the Goat Queen," said the old goat. "I shall not live much longer, but I want to eat a hundred elephants, seventy-five buffaloes, fifty tigers and twenty-five lions before I die. I've eaten the elephants, buffaloes and tigers already. Now I'm looking for lions."

The lion was terrified.

"Let me go and wash myself in the river before you eat me," he whimpered.

"I will let him go," thought the goat. "Then I can sleep peacefully in this cave. That's the best thing to do." So she agreed to the lion's last wish.

As the lion rushed down the hillside, he met a jackal.

"Ha, ha," laughed the surprised jackal. "I've never seen a frightened lion before. Why are you so scared?"

"Scared!" roared the lion. "I'm terrified! A horrible monster called the Goat Queen rushed into my cave. She had flashing eyes, a long, white beard and the sharpest horns I've ever seen. She eats lions and she wanted to eat me."

"I've never heard of a Goat Queen," said the jackal. "I'll return to the cave with you and see this monster. I think we'll be the ones having a good dinner, not her."

So the lion and the jackal went back to the cave where the goat was dozing. First she smelled them. Then, with a start, she opened her eyes and saw them.

"I will have to brave it out," she thought to herself. "That's the best thing to do." And she marched boldly outside.

"Well, Jackal," she cried. "What do you think you are doing? I ordered you to find twenty-five lions and what have you done? You've brought me one shivery, shaky lion. I shall have to eat you both for breakfast."

"You tricked me, Jackal," roared the lion. "This goat ordered you to catch me, didn't she?" He sprang at the jackal, who turned tail and ran.

"I think I had better go home now," said the goat to herself. "That's the best thing to do." And that really was the best thing to do!

THE MAYOR'S EGG

Some time ago, there was a man who found the most enormous pumpkin.

"Snakes alive!" he exclaimed. "Whatever can this be?" He smelled it, he poked it, then he picked it up and took it home to show everybody. The oldest, wisest man in the village stared at the pumpkin.

"I've lived a long time, but I've never seen anything like this," he said. The oldest, wisest woman agreed with him.

"Maybe the mayor can help us," she suggested.

The mayor took one look at the enormous pumpkin and said, "Friends, you just have to look at its shape to know what this is. There can be no doubt about it, it is an egg!"

The villagers nodded their heads. If the mayor said it was an egg, then it must be an egg. But what sort of an egg? Could it be a snake's egg? No, it was too big. They thought it might be a dragon's egg, but nobody knew what a dragon's egg looked like. Then the man who'd found the pumpkin spoke up.

"I did see a four-legged creature with a thick mane running away from the egg," he said.

"That's it then," cried the mayor. "It's a mare's egg."

"But, Mr Mayor," said the puzzled villagers, "you have never laid an egg. Mayors don't lay eggs!"

"Of course not," said the mayor crossly. "It's the egg of a mare – M.A.R.E. – a female horse."

"Oh, a horse's egg!" the villagers exclaimed. "Of course, Mr Mayor. Only a horse could lay such an enormous egg."

"What shall we do next?" the mayor asked.

"Hatch it," everybody shouted.

"How?" asked the mayor. "We have no horses to sit on it."

All the villagers sat down and thought and thought. Then the mayor said, "I have it! We must hatch the egg ourselves."

And that is just what they did! Each villager took it in turns to sit on the egg for a day. But of course nothing happened, because, as we know, the egg was not an egg at all but a pumpkin.

At last, some people from another village saw them. They laughed and shouted, "Ho, ho, mother hens! Your egg will never hatch. It's addled! In other words, it's gone rotten."

Addled! The mayor was upset. He shook the pumpkin. Then he smelled it.

"I'm sure a baby horse is moving inside," he said.

But the villagers were furious.

"We're not sitting on this egg any longer," they said. "It smells, so it must be addled."

They put the pumpkin in a wheelbarrow and everybody helped to push it to the top of a hill. Then the mayor tipped the wheelbarrow and sent the pumpkin rolling down the hill straight towards the next village!

The pumpkin rolled over and over until it hit a stone and burst open. A little rabbit dashed out of a hedge when it heard the crash. The villagers clapped and cheered.

"Look!" they cried. "There's the baby horse. It's hatched out. Let's catch it." And they ran and rolled down the hill. The mayor did not run. He knew he couldn't catch the rabbit, but he said to himself, "I knew all along there was something moving inside that egg."

TITTY MOUSE
AND
TATTY MOUSE

Titty Mouse and Tatty Mouse did everything together in their little house. If Titty Mouse ate a nut, Tatty Mouse ate a nut, and they ate their nuts together.

One day, Titty Mouse wanted a cup of tea. Then Tatty Mouse wanted a cup of tea, so they both boiled some water. Tatty Mouse poured her boiling water carefully, but Titty Mouse poured hers all over herself and was killed.

Tatty Mouse wept and wept. Her three-legged stool asked, "Tatty, why do you weep?"

"Titty's dead," sobbed Tatty, "so I weep."

"Then I'll hop," said the stool. And it hopped.

"Stool," said the broom, "why do you hop?"

"Titty's dead, Tatty weeps, so I hop," said the stool.

"Then I'll sweep," said the broom. And it swept.

"Broom," said the door, "why do you sweep?"

"Titty's dead, Tatty weeps, Stool hops, so I sweep," said the broom.

"Then I'll creak," said the door. And it creaked.

Near the house grew a big, strong oak tree.

"Door," said the tree, "why do you creak?"

"Titty's dead, Tatty weeps, Stool hops, Broom sweeps, so I creak," said the door.

"Then I'll drop all my acorns," said the oak tree. And it dropped all its acorns.

There was a blackbird sitting on a branch in the tree and it chirped, "Oak Tree, why do you drop your acorns?"

"Titty's dead, Tatty weeps, Stool hops, Broom sweeps, Door creaks, so I drop my acorns."

"Then I'll lose my shiny black feathers," said the bird. And it lost all its feathers.

A little girl was walking home, carrying a big jug of milk for her little brother and sister. As she passed under the tree, a feather floated down and tickled her nose. She looked up and saw the blackbird shivering in the tree.

"Blackbird," she said, "why do you lose your feathers?"

"Titty's dead, Tatty weeps, Stool hops, Door creaks, Oak Tree drops acorns, so I lose my feathers," said the bird.

"Then I'll spill the milk," said the little girl. And she dropped the jug and spilled the milk.

Nearby, an old farmer was perched on a ladder, making a fine haystack. When he saw the little girl spill the milk, he said, "Little Girl, whatever are you doing? Your brother and sister cannot have their supper now."

"Oh dear," said the little girl. "Titty's dead, Tatty weeps, Stool hops, Broom sweeps, Door creaks, Oak Tree drops acorns, Blackbird loses feathers, so I spill the milk."

"My word," said the old farmer, "then I'll tumble off this ladder." And he tumbled off the ladder.

When the old farmer tumbled off the ladder, the girl ran off, the bird flew away, the oak tree came crashing down and hit the door, which fell on the broom, which knocked over the stool, and poor Tatty Mouse was left somewhere inside the house, hiding in a corner.

THE HUSBAND WHO LOOKED AFTER THE HOUSE

Once upon a time, there was a man called Peter who was very cross and grumpy and was always scolding his wife.

One day, when he came home from the fields, his wife was making the dinner, but it was not quite ready.

"Why can't you ever do anything right?" shouted Peter.

His wife replied, "Don't be so angry, dear. Why don't we swap jobs tomorrow? I will work in the fields and you can look after the house." Peter agreed, so, next day, Peter's wife set off to the meadow while Peter stayed at home.

First, he decided to churn the cream into butter. After a while he began to feel thirsty, so he went down to the cellar to pour himself some beer. He had just turned the tap on the barrel when he heard a terrible noise upstairs in the kitchen. He rushed up the steps and what a sight met his eyes! There in the kitchen was the pig. It had come in from the yard, knocked over the churn and was now guzzling up the cream.

Peter shouted at the pig and gave it such a kick that it flew out of the door into the yard. Then he remembered his beer. He ran back down the cellar steps. But he was too late! Every last drop of beer had run out of the barrel on to the cellar floor.

75

Peter had to start all over again. He filled the churn with cream and churned away for a while. But then he remembered that the cow was still shut in the barn. She had not eaten a blade of grass or had a drop of water all morning.

"It'll take me an hour to take her up to the field and come home again," he thought. "While I'm gone, the butter will spoil in the churn. What shall I do?"

"I know," he said. "I'll take her up onto the roof."

(This may sound strange, but in that country the roofs of some houses were covered with grass.)

Peter's house stood close to a steep hill and he decided to lay a plank from the hill to the roof and lead the cow across. He didn't dare leave the churn this time, so he loaded it onto his back before setting off to the barn.

On his way, Peter remembered that the cow had not had a drink. So he grabbed a bucket and went to the well. But, as he leaned over the well, all the cream ran out of the churn, over his shoulders and down into the well.

"Oh dear!" shouted Peter. "What shall I do? It's nearly lunch-time and I haven't even churned the butter yet. I'd better make some soup for lunch and churn the butter later."

So he went back to the kitchen and set a pot of water on the fire. Then he remembered the cow.

"She still hasn't had anything to eat or drink, poor thing," he cried.

This time he got the water safely from the well and took it to the barn. The cow was indeed very thirsty and she quickly drank the bucket dry.

Then Peter led her up onto the roof. As soon as he got there, he began to worry about the water on the fire. He ran down to the kitchen, but all was well. Quickly, Peter cut up some carrots and some onions and threw them into the pot. Just as he had finished, he began to worry about the cow.

"What if she falls off the roof and breaks her leg?" he thought. "I'd better tie her up."

So he found a length of rope and went back onto the roof. Peter tied one end of the rope round the cow's neck, but there was nowhere to tie the other end. Then he had a brilliant idea. He slipped the end of the rope down the chimney, ran back down into the kitchen and tied the rope round his leg.

"That will keep her safe," he said to himself, feeling very pleased with his clever plan.

Now the soup was beginning to smell good. Peter stirred the onions and carrots and looked around for some beans to add to them. Just at that moment the cow slipped off the roof. As she fell, her weight dragged Peter half-way up the chimney. And there he stuck fast.

Out in the meadow, Peter's wife decided she had waited long enough for her lunch, so she set off for home. What a sight met her eyes! There was the poor cow swinging from the roof on a rope. Quick as a flash, she raised her scythe and cut through the rope. The cow landed softly on a pile of hay.

But inside the house there was a terrible crash. Peter's wife rushed into the kitchen. And what did she see? With the cow's weight gone from the rope, Peter had come tumbling down out of the chimney. There he was, upside down, in the soup pot!

"Well, that's a funny way to cook," said his wife as she hauled him out. "I think looking after the house is too difficult for you. You had better go and mow the hay tomorrow."

And after that, Peter never snarled or scolded or shouted at his wife – well, hardly ever.

MASTER OF ALL MASTERS

Long ago, servant-girls and young men went to the market-place to find work. One day, a girl called Saskia went there to look for a new master. After a time, a strange but kind-looking old man asked her to come and work for him and Saskia agreed.

"Now, Saskia," he said, "in my house I have special names for everything. You must learn them all. To start with, what will you call me?"

"Master? Mister? Sir? Whatever you like," said Saskia.

"You must call me Master of all Masters," said the man. Then he pointed to his bed and asked, "What is this called?"

"Bed? Cot? Sofa? Whatever you like, Master of all Masters," she said.

"No. That's my sleepasaurous rex," said the old man, and he pointed to his trousers. "What are these?"

"Breeches? Leggings? Pantaloons? Whatever you like, Master of all Masters."

"Crockers and gators," said the old man. "That's what they are called."

Next he pointed to his cat and asked, "What's her name?"

"Cat? Kitty? Pussy? Whatever you like, Master of all Masters," said Saskia.

"You must call her Scratchmio," said the old man. Then, as he poked the glowing fire, he asked, "What is this?"

"Fire? Coals? Flames? Whatever you like, Master of all Masters," replied Saskia.

"You must call it sizzle and pop," said the old man, and he turned to a pan of water. "What is this?"

"Water? Rain? Lemonade? Whatever you like, Master of all Masters," said Saskia, who was beginning to enjoy all this.

"No, it's called wishy-washy," said the old man. Then he waved his arms and pointed to his house. "What is this called?"

80

"House? Castle? Cottage? Whatever you like, Master of all Masters," said Saskia.

"No, I want you to call it high tipper topper," he said. He looked thoughtfully at the girl and said, "As I have special names for everything, you must have a special name too."

"Whatever you like, Master of all Masters," said the girl with a big smile.

"I shall call you Soapy Soapsuds from now on."

Well, that very night, Saskia woke with a fright. She threw on her warmest clothes, then she rushed to the old man's room. She shook him hard and shouted, "This is Soapy Soapsuds, Master of all Masters. You must leave your sleepa-saurous rex and put on your crockers and gators. Scratchmio has pulled the sizzle and pop on to the carpet. If you don't get some wishy-washy, high tipper topper will be on sizzle and pop!"

So there!

81

NAIL SOUP

One dark night, a soldier was trudging through the snow. He was cold and hungry, so he knocked on the door of a cottage near the road.

"May I come in and shelter?" he called.

An old woman came to the door.

"You can shelter for a while," she said rather unwillingly.

"Can you spare me a little food to eat?" the soldier asked.

"Oh dear," the old woman sighed. "I haven't any food in the house. I haven't eaten anything myself since yesterday. It's terrible to be so poor."

"Well, if you haven't any food, I'll just warm myself beside this hot stove," the soldier replied. He sat down and then he sniffed the air once or twice. Then, with a funny little smile, he took a nail out of his pocket.

"As you've nothing else, I suppose I could make some nail soup," he said.

The old woman stared at him.

"Nail soup? I've never heard of such a thing," she said. But she looked curiously at the nail. "I would be pleased if you would show me how to make soup out of a nail."

82

"Certainly," came the reply. "Just bring me a large pot and some water."

The old woman scuttled away and found a pot, which she filled with water. The soldier put it on the stove and dropped in the nail. The old woman's eyes almost popped out of her head when the soldier started to stir the soup with a long spoon. Then he tasted it.

"Mmm! It will be ready soon, but it's a pity it hasn't a little pepper and salt in it."

"I expect I could spare a little," the woman said, and she sprinkled some salt and pepper into the water. The soldier stirred the soup once or twice and tasted the soup again.

"Half an onion would be nice," he said.

The woman brought out a large, fat onion and the soldier dropped it into the pot. He stirred and stirred. Then he tasted the soup again.

"This is a fine soup," he murmured. "If only it had a few carrots and potatoes in it, it would be a wonderful soup."

In a flash, the old woman peeled carrots and potatoes and dropped them in the pot. By now the soup was smelling good.

"At first this was a fine soup," said the soldier, "then it was a wonderful soup. If only I had a little meat, then I could turn it into a soup fit for a king."

Once more the old woman dashed into the pantry and this time she came back with some meat!

"What a pity we haven't a nice, crusty loaf to eat with our soup," said the soldier. "But I think you said you hadn't any food in the house?"

"I might be able to find a leftover crust," said the old woman gruffly. She opened the bread bin and pulled out a freshly baked loaf!

The soldier poured the soup into two bowls and quickly fished out his nail, which he washed and put into his pocket. They had a wonderful meal in front of the fire and the old woman could not praise the soup enough.

"Well, well," she said. "I never thought anybody could make such a tasty soup out of an old nail!"

"Neither did I," whispered the soldier to himself.

HOW ISHDAKA FOUND SUMMER

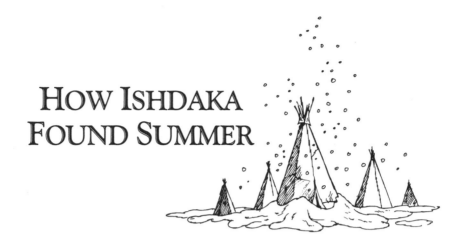

Long ago, the Wawaniki Indians had a great leader called Ishdaka. One day they went to him and said, "Please help us, Ishdaka. Giant Winter's icy breath has frozen our lands. Our fields are covered with snow and we have no food left."

So Ishdaka set off to find Giant Winter and ask him to leave the lands of the Wawaniki. He travelled for many days, but at last he came to the giant's house. The giant seemed to be friendly. He invited Ishdaka into his igloo and told him wonderful stories about Indian spirits and fairies. But all the time he was casting a frosty spell on Ishdaka, who fell into a deep sleep.

Ishdaka slept for six months. Then one day, a wild bird whispered in his ear, "Wake up, Ishdaka. You must travel south and find Summer. She is far stronger than Winter. You must find her if you want to save your people."

85

Ishdaka woke up at once and whistled a tune to call his friend the whale. The whale pushed through the ice that covered the sea and Ishdaka jumped onto his back. The whale swam south for many days. Slowly the icy waters grew warmer and Ishdaka could smell flowers and fruit. Then some dolphins whispered to him, "Do not go too close to the shore. The water is not deep enough for whales!"

"What are the dolphins saying?" asked the whale.

Ishdaka wanted to land quickly, so he replied, "They are telling us to hurry because there is a storm coming."

The whale swam faster and Ishdaka soon saw the beach. Then bump! the whale got stuck on the sand and Ishdaka was able to walk along his head onto dry land.

"Help me off here," shouted the whale.

Ishdaka was sorry for tricking his friend. He placed his feet firmly on the sand and pushed the whale as hard as he could. He

pushed and pushed until at last the whale was in deeper water and able to swim free.

Then Ishdaka set off to find Summer. He walked over warm sands until he reached a meadow. Many children were there, dancing round a beautiful girl. On her head she wore a crown of flowers and her arms were full of sheaves of corn.

"She must be Summer," thought Ishdaka. He ran between the children and persuaded Summer to help him.

Once again Ishdaka called on his friend the whale and, together, he and Summer travelled back to Winter's icy igloo. Winter was very pleased to see them. He had two people to freeze now! But, this time, Ishdaka was ready for him and he began to tell him the stories and legends of his people, the Wawaniki. As Winter listened, spellbound, Summer slowly began to melt his icy beard. She melted his ice house and the frozen rivers. Then she used her special power to wake up all the trees and flowers. Winter could do nothing to stop her.

"You see how strong I am," Summer said. "The fields are green again and the crops are growing. If you promise to return to the far north, Winter, I will leave you alone. You may visit Ishdaka's country for six months every year, but you must not be so fierce. I will stay here for the other six months to warm the people and let them grow food."

Winter agreed to the bargain. He still goes to the Wawaniki's lands every year, but he only stays for six months. When he has gone, Summer arrives and makes the land warm and fruitful once more.

THE
CAMEL'S HUMP

The camel's hump is an ugly lump
Which well you may see at the Zoo;
But uglier yet is the hump we get
From having too little to do.

Kiddies and grown-ups too-oo-oo
If we haven't enough to do-oo-oo,
We get the hump –
Cameelious hump –
The hump that is black and blue!

We climb out of bed with a frouzly head
And a snarly-yarly voice.
We shiver and scowl and we grunt and we growl
At our bath and our boots and our toys;

And there ought to be a corner for me
(And I know there is one for you)
When we get the hump –
Cameelious hump –
The hump that is black and blue!

The cure for this ill is not to sit still,
Or frowst with a book by the fire;
But to take a large hoe and a shovel also,
And dig till you gently perspire;

And then you will find that the sun and the wind,
And the Djinn of the Garden too,
        Have lifted the hump –
        The horrible hump –
The hump that is black and blue!

I get it as well as you-oo-oo
If I haven't enough to do-oo-oo!
        We all get the hump –
        Cameelious hump –
Kiddies and grown-ups too!

THE GINGERBREAD MAN

One day, an old woman was making gingerbread when she thought to herself, "I'll make a little gingerbread man. Here are some currants for his nose, his eyes and his little mouth." She put currants down his front too, for coat buttons. Then she put him on a baking tray and popped him into a nice hot oven.

Soon she heard a knock on the oven door. She opened it and out jumped the gingerbread man.

"Goodness gracious!" exclaimed the woman, and she tried to catch the gingerbread man. But he scampered past her into the garden, shouting:

"Run, run as fast as you can,
You can't catch me, I'm the gingerbread man."

The old woman's husband tried to catch him, but the gingerbread man ducked under his arm and ran out into the road, calling:

"Run, run as fast as you can,
You can't catch me, I'm the gingerbread man."

On the road he met a cow, who mooed, "Stop! I'd like to eat you." But the gingerbread man just laughed and sang:

91

"*Run, run as fast as you can,*
You can't catch me, I'm the gingerbread man."
The old woman, the old man and the cow chased after him until they met a dog. The dog barked, "Stop, Gingerbread Man! I'd like a bite of you." But the gingerbread man just shouted once again:
"*I'm faster than the old woman,*
And the old man,
And the fat cow.
Run, run as fast as you can,
You can't catch me, I'm the gingerbread man."
The gingerbread man ran on down the road, chased by the old woman, the old man, the cow and the dog. A little farther on they met a policeman.

92

"Stop!" he said sternly. "What's the trouble here?"

The gingerbread man called out as he passed:

"I'm faster than the old woman,
And the old man,
And the fat cow,
And the dog.
Run, run as fast as you can,
You can't catch me, I'm the gingerbread man."

The policeman tried to grab the gingerbread man, but he skipped away. Now the old woman, the old man, the cow, the dog and the policeman were all chasing after him. The gingerbread man turned into a field and hummed a little song:

"So many folk are chasing me,
But I'm the leader you can see."

A fox who was lying in the grass, said to himself, "That gingerbread man smells good." Then he saw the old woman, the old man, the cow, the dog and the policeman running after the gingerbread man. So he joined the chase too.

Suddenly the gingerbread man stopped. He had come to a wide, rushing river. The gingerbread man couldn't swim across because he would melt in the water. What was he going to do? Just then the cunning fox raced up to him and whispered, "Jump on my back. I'll take you across the river."

So the gingerbread man jumped onto the fox's back.

"You'd better move to my head, little man," the fox said as he swam across, "or you'll get wet." So the gingerbread man moved along to the fox's head.

Soon the water was so deep that even the fox's head was getting splashed.

"Sit on my nose," the fox said, "you will be dry there." So the gingerbread man slid down onto the fox's nose. SNIP SNAP! went the fox, and the gingerbread man disappeared. But where did he go? The fox knows!

THE
HAPPY SPINNER

There was once a girl who hated spinning. This annoyed her
mother and one day she spanked her daughter, making her
weep and wail. Now it so happened that the queen was passing
by and she asked why the girl was crying so loudly.

The girl's mother didn't want to admit that her daughter
wouldn't spin, so before her daughter could say anything, she
said, "All my daughter wants to do is spin, spin, spin and I
haven't enough money to buy flax for her."

"I love the sound of a spinning-wheel," said the queen.
"There's plenty of flax at the palace. Why don't you let your
daughter come with me and she can spin all day long."

The queen took the poor girl to her palace and showed her
six rooms filled with flax.

"Here you are, my dear," said the queen. "When you've
spun all this, you may marry my son." Then she left the room.

"Oh dear," wailed the girl. "I hate spinning! I'll never
finish this in a hundred years. Whatever shall I do?" She was so
upset that she sat down and did nothing!

That night, the queen came back and she was surprised to
see that all six rooms were still full of flax.

"Why haven't you started your spinning?" she demanded.

"I've been thinking of my mother all day," the girl sighed.

"Quite right and proper," replied the queen, "but you must work hard tomorrow."

Next day, the girl still could not bring herself to start spinning. As she stood by the window, looking into the street, she saw a strange old woman walking by. She was quite the strangest person the girl had ever seen. She had a wide, flat foot, her bottom lip hung down over her chin and she had an enormous thumb.

"What's the matter?" called the old woman when she saw the girl's sad face.

The girl told the old woman her sad story. When she had finished, the old woman said, "I'll come inside and help you, but you must promise to invite me to your wedding and let me sit near the prince."

"Of course," the girl promised as she ran to open the door.

The old woman started work by pulling out pieces of flax and spinning the wheel with her big right foot. The spinning wheel made thread, which she wet with her thick bottom lip. Then she rolled the thread into balls with her huge thumb. Treading, wetting, rolling she went until the six rooms were empty. She left the girl just before the queen arrived.

"What wonderful spinning," exclaimed the queen. "I will order your wedding feast at once. My son is lucky to get such a hard-working wife."

Then the girl asked, "May I invite my cousin to the wedding? She has been very kind to me and I would like her to sit at our table."

"Certainly," replied the queen, smiling.

On the wedding day, the old woman arrived dressed in a

frilly lace dress. The prince was surprised to see her, but he talked to her politely and then said, "If you don't mind me asking, how did you get such a big foot?"

"Treading the wheel. Treading the wheel," came the old woman's reply.

"And what made your lip so long?" asked the prince.

"Wetting the thread. Wetting the thread," answered the old woman.

"And what made your thumb so enormous?"

"Twisting the thread. Twisting the thread."

"If spinning makes you look like that," said the horrified prince, "my beautiful wife must never touch a spinning wheel!"

And, to her delight, she never did!

SWEET PORRIDGE

Once upon a time, a girl and her little brother lived with their mother in a tiny cottage. They were very poor, so they often went to bed without any supper. But then the day came when there was nothing left to eat in the cottage, not even a crumb.

"We'll go to the woods and look for nuts and berries," said the children, and off they went.

They had not been hunting for long, when they met an old woman whose eyes twinkled merrily.

"Well, my dears, you look very thin and hungry to me," she said. The children nodded sadly, then watched as the old woman pulled a little black pan out of her skirt pocket.

"What a funny place to keep a pan," whispered the little boy to his sister.

"Ah, but this is a special pan," laughed the old woman, and she gave it to the little girl. "Take it home and put it on the stove. If you say, 'Cook, little pan, cook,' it will hubble and bubble and cook lovely sweet porridge for you all. As soon as you have eaten enough, just say, 'Stop, little pan, stop,' and it will stop cooking until you want some more."

The two children raced back home and showed the pan to their mother. The little girl put the pan on the stove and, sure enough, that little black pan made hot porridge whenever they needed it.

One day, the girl went out by herself. While she was away, her brother grew hungry. He begged his mother for some porridge. She put the pan on the stove and said, "Cook, little pan, cook." At once there was a nice warm smell in the kitchen and the two of them enjoyed a good meal.

"We'd better stop the pan cooking now," the mother said. But, oh dear me! She could not remember the words. The pan went on and on cooking. It cooked until porridge ran over the top of the stove and down the sides. It cooked until the little cottage was filled right up with porridge. It cooked until porridge flowed out through the windows into the garden. It went on cooking, cooking, cooking until the whole street was full of porridge. The neighbours were alarmed.

"Hubble, bubble, stop this load of trouble!" they cried. But the little black pan just went on bubbling. Soon the porridge had spread over the fields.

"Sniff, sniff, what queer new food is this?" thought the farm animals.

At last the girl came home. Quick as a flash she cried, "Stop, little pan, stop."

The pan stopped cooking at once. But the cows, the pigs, the horses, the sheep and ALL the people had to eat a lot of porridge before they could get back to their houses.

HARE THE HERO

There was once a little hare who was always frightened. Pitter patter raindrops, falling leaves, a mouse nibbling a nut – all these made him jump. And when hares jump, they jump really high!

The other hares were scared of bears and wolves, but creaking trees and falling snow didn't bother them. They called this little hare Shaker and teased him all day long.

At last the little hare grew tired of their jokes.

"You're a big hare now," he told himself; "a grown up hare, in fact. You must stop this shivering and shaking NOW."

"Why are you talking to yourself, Shaker?" asked another hare as he walked past.

"Stop calling me Shaker," replied the little hare. "I'm not shaking. I'm not scared. I'm not going to be frightened of anything any more. I'll never, ever, ever shake again."

And he ran off through the forest, calling out, "I'm brave. I'm very, very brave."

"What about the bear?" asked his friends when they caught up with him. "Aren't you frightened of him?"

"Pooh! Who's scared of an old bear?" laughed Shaker.

"Well, what about the wolf then?"

"That miserable creature! He'd better watch out for me," said Shaker, stamping his foot – boom, boom.

At that moment, a wolf came slinking by. He heard the hares chatting and he licked his lips.

"Oh good! It looks like hare for supper," he thought.

"And there's something else," Shaker yelled. "After I've gobbled up the first wolf who gets in my way, I want a new name – Hare the Hero."

The wolf snarled.

"A hare eat a wolf! What nonsense," he said, and crept closer, ready to pounce on his supper.

Just then Shaker saw the wolf. He was terrified and shook from head to foot. He got such a fright that he jumped high into the air and landed on the wolf's back. Well, this frightened him even more, so he gave another tremendous leap and ran away just as fast as he could run.

He ran and ran. When he became hot, he thought it was the wolf's hot breath on his tail. When stones rattled under his paws, he felt certain the wolf's teeth were snapping at his tail.

At last he could run no farther and he crawled under the thickest bush he could find to hide.

But where was the wolf? Well, he hadn't been chasing the little hare at all. When the hare landed on his back, the wolf had heard the crack, crack of Shaker's chattering teeth.

"There's a hunter with a gun after me," he thought, and so he fled in the other direction to save his life! He had run far away, right out of the forest.

The other hares were astonished.

"Did you see how Shaker jumped on the wolf?" they exclaimed. "He was so brave. We can't call him Shaker now."

But where was Shaker? He was still under the bush, puffing and panting. When his friends found him, they patted him on the back and cheered.

"Well done, Hare the Hero. The wolf has gone. You weren't boasting. You really are brave."

"Brave? Me?" questioned Shaker.

The other hares told him how the wolf had run away. When they had finished, Shaker laughed and said, "Of course I'm brave. You're all shakers now."

BEAUTY

Long ago, in a little cottage, there lived a pretty girl and her mother. The girl's friends called her Beauty, because not only did she have a beautiful face, but she was also kind and helpful too.

One fine day, the prince was riding through the village and he saw Beauty walking along the road with a scarf over her face. Turning to his servant, he said, "Why is that girl covering her face with a scarf?"

"She is very beautiful," his servant replied, "but she is also modest and shy. That is why she covers her face with a scarf."

The prince was amazed at such modesty and immediately fell in love with Beauty.

"Take this ring to her," he said to his servant, "and ask her to meet me under yonder oak tree."

Beauty agreed to meet the prince, but was astonished when the prince begged her to marry him.

"But, Sire!" she exclaimed. "You do not know me. Besides, your father, the king, would never allow you to marry a poor girl." And with that she ran home.

Next day, the prince sent Beauty a silver necklace and

again asked her to meet him under the tree. She still kept her face covered, but the prince still begged her to marry him.

"I cannot say yes," she replied, "your father would be so angry." And off she ran.

On the third day, the prince sent Beauty a gown sparkling with diamonds and went to wait under the tree. This time, when Beauty arrived, her face was uncovered. The prince was struck by her loveliness.

"You are even more beautiful than I imagined," he told her. "I will ask you to marry me every day until you say yes."

After many days, Beauty at last agreed to marry the prince, for she had fallen in love with him too.

Now, when the king heard the news, he was furious and he ordered his men to burn down the cottage where Beauty and her mother lived. This made them so poor that Beauty was forced to look for work. So she borrowed some boy's clothing, pinned up her beautiful, long hair and became a servant at the king's palace.

"What is your name, boy?" asked the king.

"Unlucky," replied Beauty.

So helpful and cheerful was he, that it was not long before Unlucky became the king's favourite servant.

Meanwhile, the prince was sure that Beauty had been burned to death, but he could not forget her and he refused to marry anyone else.

Eventually, the king ordered him to marry a princess from another country. There was nothing the prince could do and he set off with his father to visit the princess.

As they were riding along, they heard someone singing.

"Who is singing that lovely song?" asked the prince.

"Oh, that's my servant, Unlucky," said the king as the prince listened carefully to the words.

"Beauty was a girl I knew,

Sadly, Beauty was Unlucky too."

The prince turned round, rode up to his father's favourite servant and immediately recognized his beloved Beauty! Taking

106

Beauty with him, he returned to his father, hardly able to conceal his joy.

"Your Majesty," he said, "before I marry this princess that you have chosen for me, I wish to ask you one thing. If I have a friend and then I make a new friend, should I forget my first friend?"

"Certainly not," said the king, "that would be very unkind and ungrateful."

"Well," the prince laughed, "the princess is my new friend, but here is my first friend." And he turned to Beauty and took her by the hand.

"But he's my servant!" exclaimed the king.

"She is my beautiful bride," cried the prince, pulling off Beauty's cap and letting her long, golden hair flow down.

And so, a few days later, Beauty and the prince were married. The king soon came to love the poor girl who had married his son, and within a month had invited Beauty's mother to live with them in the palace.

NAUGHTY DAISY

There was once a cow and this cow's name was DAISY.
Daisy the cow lived in a field, with NINE other cows.
(MooO-OO-OO. MooO-OO-OO.)

Every afternoon, when the farmer came to fetch the cows
home to bed, that naughty Daisy would run away and HIDE.

And her big, fat body would shake WITH LAUGHTER.

(Hoo-Hoo! Hoo-Hoo!)

NAUGHTY DAISY!

When the farmer called, "Daisy, where are you?" she
would shake and shake with laughter.

NAUGHTY DAISY!

Day after day, when he collected the cows, he would count
them as they went through the gate:

1, 2, 3, 4, 5, 6, 7, 8, 9!

Nine good cows, but oh dear! NO DAISY AGAIN.

So: first he looked behind a tree. *NO DAISY.*

Then he looked behind the water trough. *NO DAISY.*

Then he looked in the ditch. *NO DAISY.*

Then he looked under the may trees. NO DAISY.

Then at last, he looked behind the bush.

"Hoo-oo. Hoo!"

Shaking and shaking.

"WHY! THERE you are, naughty Daisy," the farmer said. "You make me hunt for you, every day! What can I do about you?"

And he thought and thought.

"I have an idea!" the farmer said one day. "I'll soon put a stop to Daisy's game!"

And that night, when Daisy was fast asleep, he hung a big bell round her neck.

Next day, he went as usual to bring home the cows, and when he counted them as they came through the gate there were:

1, 2, 3, 4, 5, 6, 7, 8, 9, – but NO DAISY!

Nine good cows but NO DAISY!

But he didn't go to look for her. No. He listened.

And coming from behind a bush, he heard, "Cling, clang, cling, clang."

It was the bell clanging as Daisy's big, fat body shook and shook with laughter! "Hoo-Hoo! Hoo-Hoo!"

CLING CLANG! CLING CLANG!

And although Daisy wasn't at all pleased at being found so quickly, the farmer was very happy.

Now he could *hear* where she was, because of the bell round her neck!

He would never, never have to hunt again for … NAUGHTY DAISY.

THE GIANT WHO THREW TANTRUMS

At the foot of Thistle Mountain lay a village. In the village lived a little boy who liked to go walking. One Saturday afternoon he was walking in the woods when he was startled by a terrible noise.

He scrambled quickly behind a bush.

Before long a huge giant came stamping down the path.

He looked upset.

"Tanglebangled ringlepox!" the giant bellowed. He banged his head against a tree until the leaves shook off like snowflakes. "Franglewhangled whippersnack!" the giant roared. Yanking up the tree, he whirled it around his head and knocked down twenty-seven other trees.

Muttering to himself, he stalked up the path towards the top of Thistle Mountain.

The little boy hurried home.

"I just saw a giant throwing a tantrum!" he told everyone in the village.

They only smiled.

"There's no such thing as a giant," the mayor assured him.

"He knocked down twenty-seven trees," said the little boy.

"Must have been a tornado," the weatherman said with a nod. "Happens around here all the time."

The next Saturday afternoon the little boy again went walking. Before long he heard a terrible noise. Quick as lightning, he slipped behind a tree.

Soon the same giant came storming down the path. He still looked upset.

"Pollywogging fizzlesnatch!" he yelled. Throwing himself down, he pounded the ground with both fists.

Boulders bounced like hailstones.

Scowling, the giant puckered his lips into an 'O'.

He drew in his breath sharply. It sounded like somebody slurping soup.

"Pooh!" he cried.

Grabbing his left foot with both hands, the giant hopped on his right foot up the path towards the top of Thistle Mountain.

The little boy hurried home.

"That giant's at it again," he told everyone. "He threw such a tantrum that the ground trembled!"

"Must have been an earthquake," the police chief said. "Happens around here sometimes."

The next Saturday afternoon the little boy again went walking. Before long he heard a frightening noise.

He dropped down behind a rock.

Soon the giant came fuming down the path. When he reached the little boy's rock, he puckered his lips into an 'O'. He drew in his breath sharply with a loud, rushing wind sound.

"Phooey!" he cried. "I *never* get it right!"

The giant held his breath until his face turned blue and his eyes rolled up. "Fozzlehumper backawacket!" he panted. Then

he lumbered up the path towards the top of Thistle Mountain.

The little boy followed him. Up and up and up he climbed to the very top of Thistle Mountain.

There he discovered a huge cave. A surprising sound was coming from it. The giant was crying!

"All I want is to whistle," he sighed through his tears. "But every time I try, it comes out wrong!"

The little boy had just learned to whistle. He knew how hard it could be. He stepped inside the cave.

The giant looked surprised. "How did *you* get here?"

"I know what you're doing wrong," the little boy said.

When the giant heard that, he leaned down and put his hands on his knees.

"Tell me at once!" he begged.

"You have to stop throwing tantrums," the little boy told him.

"I promise!" said the giant, who didn't want anyone to think he had poor manners.

"Pucker your lips…" the little boy said.

"I always do!" the giant assured him.

"Then blow," the little boy added.

"Blow?"

"Blow."

The giant looked as if he didn't believe it. He puckered his lips into an 'O'. He blew. Out came a long, low whistle. It sounded like a railway engine. The giant smiled.

He shouted, "I whistled! Did you hear that? I whistled!"

Taking the little boy's hand, he danced in a circle.

"You're a good friend," the giant said.

"Thank you," said the little boy. "Perhaps some time we can whistle together. But just now I have to go. It's my suppertime."

The giant stood before his cave and waved goodbye.

The little boy seldom saw the giant after that. But the giant kept his promise about not throwing tantrums.

"We never have earthquakes," the mayor liked to say.

"Haven't had a tornado in ages," the weatherman would add.

Now and then they heard a long, low whistle somewhere in the distance.

"Must be a train," the police chief would say.

But the little boy knew his friend the giant was walking up the path towards the top of Thistle Mountain – whistling.

115

THUNDER AND LIGHTNING'S NEW HOME

At one time, many hundreds of years ago, Lightning and Thunder lived upon the Earth. Lightning was a boy with a wicked temper. He struck anybody he didn't like and sometimes set fire to their houses. His mother, Thunder, shouted at him, but her loud, angry voice deafened everybody and only made the trees shake.

At last people began to grumble to the king.

"We are tired of Lightning's temper and Thunder's shouts," they said.

"You'd better live outside the village," the king said to Thunder and Lightning. "Then you cannot upset anyone."

Everything was quiet for a time, then Lightning started burning houses and trees again and Thunder scolded him with her loudest, thundery voice.

"Thunder and Lightning are still bothering us," the people complained to the king.

The king grew angry when he heard this.

"Thunder and Lightning," he said, "stop annoying everybody. Take yourselves off to the mountains and do not show yourselves here again."

Thunder and Lightning were furious. Their eyes flashed, but to everyone's surprise they obeyed and moved off, rumbling and grumbling.

It was peaceful then in the village, but Lightning wanted revenge. One day, he crept back down the mountainside. When he reached the village, he crackled and hissed and set the farmers' corn alight. He kicked tall trees until they split in two. He set fire to the haystacks and farm houses, and even killed cows and horses in the fields.

Thunder came after her wicked son. She shouted and bellowed, and frightened the people. She shouted so loudly that the ground shook, but Lightning took no notice. He went on flashing and crackling for hours and hours. Thunder screamed and roared until, at last, both of them were tired out.

The people of the village could take it no longer and they rushed off to tell the king.

"You must send Thunder and Lightning far away," they said. "We do not want them anywhere near us."

The king thought and thought. Then he ordered Thunder and Lightning to stand before him.

"Lightning," he said sternly, "you have been very wicked. As for you, Thunder, your big voice frightens us all. From now on you must both live in the sky."

Thunder and Lightning begged him to relent.

"I'll never be bad-tempered again," promised Lightning.

"And I'll speak softly," Thunder said.

"You'll never be able to keep these promises," the people said. "You've burned our fields and our houses. We cannot forgive you."

118

"How can you put us up into the sky?" hissed Lightning rudely, his eyes flashing.

"Wait and see," said the king.

They did not have to wait long. Hundreds of birds came flocking down – parakeets from the forest, long-legged flamingoes, pelicans and vultures. They cackled and squawked. Then they picked mother and son up with their claws and beaks and held them tightly. Up, up, up the birds flew, high above the clouds, and there they left Thunder and Lightning.

The king and the people were sure they would never be troubled again. But Lightning still loses his temper sometimes and sends bright, fiery flashes down to Earth. And a little later, Thunder roars at him. Have you ever heard her?

119

TEENY-WEENY

Teeny-Weeny was busy sweeping the floor in her little cottage when she found ten bright, shining pennies.

"That's lucky," she said to herself. "What shall I buy with these ten pennies?" And she sat down by the fire to think about what she could buy.

"I know," she thought. "I'll go to market and I'll buy a pig. Then I'll have plenty of bacon and ham to eat in the winter."

She put on her bonnet and off she went to the market, where she bought a fine pig for ten pennies. She tied a piece of rope round its neck and led it back to her little house. But when she got home, she realized that there was nowhere to keep the pig except on the clean floor under her kitchen table. But the pig would not stay there and Teeny-Weeny soon got tired of chasing it round and round her kitchen.

"I'm afraid I'll have to take you back to the market and sell you," she told the pig.

When she got to the market, Teeny-Weeny could only sell the pig for five pennies.

"What shall I buy with my five pennies?" she wondered. "I know! I've always wanted a little black cat, so that is what I'll buy." She wandered about until she spotted a fine black cat. Quickly, she paid her five pennies and carried the cat home.

When she was inside her cottage, Teeny-Weeny remembered that she had no milk. The cat mewed and mewed. She would not stop and she would not eat anything else.

"I will have to take you back to the market and sell you," said Teeny-Weeny, so she set off back to the market once again. This time, nobody would give her more than two pennies for her noisy cat.

"I only have two pennies now. What can I buy with them?" Teeny-Weeny asked herself as she wandered round the market. Then she saw a pretty bird.

"That's it!" she exclaimed. "A bird will sing and keep me company." So she bought the singing bird and set off home.

The bird perched on her finger, but they had not gone very far when they passed some trees. At once the bird flew up into the tree tops!

"Well, those ten pennies weren't so lucky after all," said Teeny-Weeny. "I'd better hurry back home and finish cleaning the floor." And that is just what she did!

THE THREE BILLY GOATS GRUFF

Once upon a time, on the far side of a river, there was a field of rich, green grass. But no animal dared to cross the bridge over the river to eat the grass because a wicked troll with fierce eyes and big teeth lived under the bridge. He hated people and animals and, if anybody tried to cross to the field, he would jump out and gobble them up!

One fine summer's day, the three Billy Goats Gruff looked across the river.

"The grass looks so green over there. Why don't we cross the river and eat some?" they said to one another. So they polished their horns, combed their long, white beards and trotted up to the bridge.

The troll was resting under the bridge when he heard a trip-trap, trip-trap over his head.

"Who is that?" he demanded.

Small Billy Goat Gruff was half-way over the bridge. He called out in his teeny-weeny voice, "It's only me, Small Billy Goat Gruff."

"You'll make a good dinner," roared the troll. "I'm coming to eat you."

"Oh no!" pleaded Small Billy Goat Gruff. "Don't eat me. My brother, Middle-sized Billy Goat Gruff, will be coming soon. He is much plumper than I am and would make a far better dinner. Why don't you eat him instead?"

"Very well," muttered the troll, and he let Small Billy Goat Gruff go trip-trap across the bridge to the field.

Soon the troll heard the noise of someone walking trip-trap, trip-trap over his head.

"Who is that?" he roared.

"It's only me, Middle-sized Billy Goat Gruff," said the goat in a middle-sized voice.

"You'll make a good dinner," the troll sneered. "I'm coming to eat you."

"Oh no! Don't eat me," said Middle-sized Billy Goat Gruff. "If you let me eat the grass in the field, I'll be much fatter tomorrow. Why don't you eat Big Billy Goat Gruff today."

"Very well," scowled the troll, and he let Middle-sized Billy Goat Gruff go trip-trap across the bridge. Then he settled down to wait for Big Billy Goat Gruff.

At last he heard a very loud trip-trap, trip-trap coming over the bridge.

"Who is that?" he bellowed.

"It's me, Big Billy Goat Gruff," the goat answered in a big, deep voice.

"You'll make a good dinner," the troll roared. "I'm coming to eat you."

"Oh no, you're not," grinned Big Billy Goat Gruff. "I have sharp, curly horns and I'll toss you into the air."

The troll was furious. He jumped up onto the bridge and rushed at Big Billy Goat Gruff. But Big Billy Goat Gruff was waiting for him. He lowered his head and charged at the troll, and hit him right in the middle with his curly horns.

The troll flew high into the air and fell Splash! into the river. He was carried away by the water and was never ever seen again.

Big Billy Goat Gruff went trip-trap across the bridge to join his two brothers. They munched the rich, green grass happily all day long and soon grew very fat.

THE OLD WOMAN OF THE FOREST

Long ago, a servant-girl was travelling in a coach with her mistress and some other servants. They were passing through a dark forest when, suddenly, some robbers jumped out and turned the coach over. The servant-girl was thrown into some bushes, but her mistress and all the other servants were killed by the wicked bandits.

When the robbers had gone, the terrified girl crept out of the bushes. Finding herself all alone, she wandered farther and farther into the forest until night-time. At last she could not walk another step, so she settled down under a tree to rest.

After a few minutes, a white dove fluttered down beside her. It dropped a tiny golden key in her lap and said, "This key will turn the lock in the tree. Open the door and you will never be hungry."

The girl looked carefully and, sure enough, there in the trunk was a tiny door with a lock. The key fitted perfectly and, when she opened the door, she found milk and bread. She ate a good supper, but then she began to feel sleepy.

"I wish I had a proper bed to sleep in," she said.

Down flew the dove with another golden key.

"Open the next tree," it cooed, "and you will find a soft place to sleep."

When the servant-girl opened the second tree, she found a pretty bed, so she snuggled down and fell fast asleep.

Next morning, the dove flew down and dropped yet another key into the girl's lap.

"Unlock the third tree and you will find some clothes to wear," it said.

Once more the girl did as she was told, and there, inside the tree, she found some clothes. And what fine clothes they were, covered with sparkling jewels!

Now the girl had somewhere to sleep and plenty of food and clothes. She decided to build a little shelter out of branches and she lived safely in the forest for many months.

One day, the dove flew down and said to the servant-girl, "Will you do something to help me?"

"Gladly," replied the servant-girl.

The dove led her to a little house and said, "Go inside and you will see an old woman. Do not speak to her, but walk past her to a door. Open the door and you will see a big table covered with gold and silver rings. You will find diamonds, emeralds and rubies too, but do not touch them. Look for a plain copper ring and bring it to me as fast as you can."

The girl agreed and walked into the house, where an old woman said roughly, "What do you want?"

But the girl said nothing and walked across to the door.

The old woman grabbed her skirt.

"You can't go in there," she screamed, "unless I say so."

But the girl tugged her skirt free and carried on walking into the room. She was dazzled by thousands of shining rings, all made of gold and silver, but she could not find the plain copper ring that she was looking for. Then she saw the old woman creeping out of the room, carrying a bird cage. The girl snatched the cage from her and saw a bird inside with a copper ring in its beak. Seizing the ring, she ran back into the forest as fast as she could. The servant-girl waited under her tree and it was not long before she thought she felt the dove's soft feathers on her neck. She turned round, but, to her surprise, she saw a handsome young prince.

"That old woman turned me into a dove," he said. "But you have broken the spell by taking the copper ring."

All at once, the trees began to turn into horses and servants. They too had been bewitched by the old woman. The prince then took the girl back to his palace and, a few days later, they were married, amidst great celebrations.

Pulled Out
Of The Water

Long, long ago, the Israelites lived happily in Egypt. But one day, a cruel man became pharaoh, King of Egypt, and he hated the Israelites.

"There are too many Israelites in Egypt now," he said to himself, "and they are strong too. One day they may take over Egypt. I'd better get rid of them." So he issued a decree that every baby boy born into an Israelite family should be killed and thrown into the river Nile.

The pharaoh's soldiers searched all the Israelite houses and they tossed every baby boy that they found into the river. But one woman from the Levi family was determined to save her new-born son. So she hid him away and nobody saw him for three months.

The baby grew big and strong and noisy! Soon the poor mother could hide him no longer. But she knew that if the soldiers found her baby, they would kill him. So she set to work and wove a basket out of rushes. She covered the rushes with thick clay mixed with oils to stop any water getting inside. Then she made a tightly fitting lid. Gently, she put her baby inside the basket and secretly went down to the river. She

floated the basket on the water and went home sadly, praying that the river would carry her baby to safety.

Now her daughter, Miriam, had followed her down to the river. Miriam decided to watch and see what would happen to her little brother.

Just then, the pharaoh's daughter came with her slaves to bathe at the water's edge. The princess moved some rushes to one side and saw the basket. She asked her slaves to bring it to her. How surprised she was to find a baby inside! The baby started to cry when he heard voices and the princess said, "Oh dear, this baby is an Israelite. My father's soldiers will kill him if they find him. But if I adopt him, he will be safe."

At that moment Miriam came out from her hiding place.

"I know a kind woman who could nurse this baby for you," she said.

"Please bring her to me at once," said the princess.

Miriam ran home and fetched the woman, who was, of course, her own mother.

"I will pay you well if you look after this baby for me," the pharaoh's daughter said to her.

Miriam's mother was overjoyed to carry her own son safely home again. She looked after him well and, when he was older, the princess took him to live in her palace. She called him Moses, which means 'pulled out of the water'.

THE COCK, THE MOUSE
AND
THE LITTLE RED HEN

A cock, a mouse and a little red hen lived in a pretty cottage by a river. In a tumbledown den on the other side, lived a fox with his three noisy sons. One day, the young foxes barked, "We're hungry. We'd like a cock or a hen for dinner."

"Well," said their father, "I'll go to that cottage over the river and catch the cock, the mouse and the little red hen. They'll make a good dinner." So he picked up a sack and set off.

In the pretty cottage, the little red hen was getting breakfast ready.

"Who will fetch sticks for the fire?" she asked.

"Not I," said the cock.

"Not I," said the mouse.

"Then I'll fetch them myself," said the little red hen, and she went out.

"Who will fill the kettle?" asked the little red hen, when she returned with the sticks.

"Not I," said the cock.

"Not I," said the mouse.

"Then I'll do it myself," said the little red hen, and she went to fetch some water.

"Who will cook the breakfast?" asked the little red hen, when the kettle was singing merrily on the fire.

"Not I," said the cock.

"Not I," said the mouse.

"Then I'll do it myself," said the little red hen, and she began to cook.

The cock and the mouse ate a huge breakfast and then went to sleep in their chairs. But the little red hen went upstairs to make the beds.

A few minutes later, the fox crept up to the house and peeped through the window. The cock and the mouse were still asleep! But, when the fox opened the door, the cock woke up with a start.

"Cock-a-doodle-do," he crowed, but the fox quickly popped him into his sack.

Then the mouse woke up.

"Squeak, squeak," he went, but the fox popped him into his sack too.

The little red hen heard the hullabaloo. She rushed downstairs and the fox popped her into his sack with the others. Then he tied the top of his sack with some string, slung it over his shoulder and set off home.

"I wish I'd helped you with the housework," said the cock. "Then I wouldn't have been asleep when the fox came."

"Yes," said the mouse, "it's all our fault."

"Don't worry," said the little red hen, "I still have my little sewing bag."

Soon the fox decided to rest. He sat down under a tree, but the sun was hot and he fell asleep.

Then the little red hen opened her bag and pulled out a pair of scissors and a needle and cotton. Snip, snap! She cut a tiny hole in the sack just big enough for the mouse to jump out.

"Quick," whispered the little red hen. "Find a stone as big as yourself and put it in the sack."

Again the scissors went snip, snap as the little red hen made a bigger hole. Out flew the cock. He too found a stone as big as himself and put it in the sack. Finally, the little red hen jumped out of the sack and found a stone as big as herself. She put it in the sack, then she quickly mended the hole with her needle and cotton. And before long, the three of them were safely back home.

Not long after, the fox woke up. He picked up his sack and began to cross the river to get to his den. He thought the sack was rather heavier than before, but he carried on anyway. Then, suddenly, he slipped. He did not want to let go of the sack, so the heavy stones pulled him down, down, under the water and he was never seen again.

Meanwhile, the cock and the mouse were so grateful to the little red hen for saving their lives that they promised to help her with the housework every day. And that evening, the cock found sticks for the fire, the mouse filled the kettle with water, but the little red hen sat down for a change and relaxed.

135

THE ELFIN KNIGHT

In a faraway country, there was once a beautiful girl called Katherina who lived with her mother and father in a splendid castle. One sunny day, Katherina was wandering in the nearby woods when she saw a bush covered with roses. The roses smelled so sweet that she picked one. At once, a handsome young man appeared from behind a tree.

"How dare you pick the roses?" he asked angrily.

Katherina dropped the rose with a start.

"I'm sorry," she said. "I didn't mean to upset anybody."

The young man saw that he had frightened the beautiful girl and spoke more gently.

"It is my job to guard these woods," he explained. "But now I see how beautiful you are, I'll gladly give you all the roses you want." And he picked a red rose and gave it to her.

"Thank you," said Katherina, blushing slightly. "What is your name?"

"My name is Tarquin," replied the young man proudly.

"The Elfin Knight!" she exclaimed. "I've heard of you."

"Do not be afraid of me," he said. "Let us sit down on this grassy bank and I will tell you my story."

136

So they sat down and Tarquin began: "I was not born an elfin knight but a mortal man. I used to love to ride in the woods. One day, as I was riding with my friends, I felt a cold wind blowing. Suddenly I felt very tired and my eyes would not stay open. My friends rode away and I fell asleep under a tree. When I woke up, I discovered that the Elf Queen had kidnapped me. She put a spell on me, so now I must guard these woods all day and go back to Elfland at night."

"Is there any way I can help you break this spell?" asked Katherina.

"There is one way," said Tarquin slowly, "but it will be very dangerous. Tonight is Hallowe'en, when the elves and fairies gather. Go to the castle gate at midnight and watch out for me. I will be riding a pure white horse and I will be wearing a gold crown. Run over to me and hold me very tightly. The Elf Queen will use her spells to try to make you let me go. But hold on, whatever happens."

Katherina ran back to the castle. That night she went to bed as usual, but, just before midnight, she dressed warmly and crept down to the castle gates. She crouched down in the shadows and waited. Soon she saw the elfin procession appear, led by the Elf Queen. In the middle of the procession was a white horse whose rider was wearing a gold crown.

Katherina ran out. She pulled Tarquin off his horse and held on to him tightly. The Elf Queen galloped up angrily and immediately whispered a spell. Tarquin changed into a hairy spider! But Katherina did not let go. The Elf Queen cast another spell. This time, the spider turned into a slithery snake, but Katherina coiled it round her hands. Then the Elf Queen whispered horribly. At once the snake changed into a red-hot poker that burned into Katherina's hands. The brave girl did not say a word but clutched the poker as tightly as she could.

The Elf Queen was beaten! She galloped away in a rage and the red-hot poker changed back into the handsome knight. He kissed Katherina's blistered hands.

"Your love and courage have saved me," he said.

"And your kiss has healed my hands," laughed Katherina. Then they walked hand in hand into the castle.

KANGAROO JOEY FINDS HIS SHADOW

"I shan't get up," said Kangaroo Joey.

"Yes, you must," his mother scolded. "Up! At once! Do you hear? Get up."

Joey climbed from his mother's pouch.

"It's cold and nasty out here," he grumbled. "I'm only a *little* Kangaroo."

"Don't be a baby," smiled Kangaroo Mother. "You're a big Joey now. You weigh down my pocket. You must learn to hop on your own strong legs, because *I* can't carry you all the time."

Kangaroo Mother leapt in the air. Then down she came to the ground. Thump!

"You see?" she said. "Like that! It's easy."

"Uh!" said Joey. "Huh!" And he jumped.

But he fell on his ears in a clump of grass.

"No, I don't like it," he said. "I shan't do it."

139

Kangaroo Mother did not spank him. She had spanked him before, and it did no good. So she and Joey ate grass for breakfast, while the sun came up and warmed their backs.

Then Kangaroo Mother said: "Climb in my pocket. I'll carry you to smoother grass. Then you can practise your jumps again."

Joey smiled as he climbed in her pouch, because he meant to stay there, for ever.

Kangaroo Mother leapt and thudded, and Joey decided to go to sleep.

But all at once he saw the shadow.

"Look!" he shouted, pointing a paw. And he nearly fell out of his mother's pocket.

When Kangaroo Mother leapt in the air, the shadow slid on the ground below them, and when she thudded down to the ground, the shadow lay still, quietly waiting.

"Slide and stop," sang Kangaroo Joey. "Slide and stop. It's following us."

By the time they reached the smoother grass, Kangaroo Joey was wriggling with laughter.

"That shadow has followed us, slide and stop, slide and stop. I think it likes us."

"I am sure it likes *me*," said Kangaroo Mother. "It's my very own shadow. That's why it follows me."

"Oh!" said Joey. "I wish it were mine. Can't I borrow it, just for today?"

Kangaroo Mother smiled, and said: "No. It is much too big for you, Joey. You must find your own shadow, to fit your own size. It is waiting for you, there on the grass."

"*I* can't see it," said Kangaroo Joey, screwing up his eyes. "Where is it?"

"Get out and look," said Kangaroo Mother.

Joey tumbled out of her pouch, and sat on the patch of sunlit grass. And there behind him, quietly waiting, was a small black shadow, all his own.

"I like it," said Joey. "And I think it likes me."

He hopped, and his shadow slid beneath him. Down he came, plop! And his shadow lay still.

"Good! I've got you, shadow," said Joey. "You can't get away. I'm sitting on you. Now, come along, shadow. I'm going to hop. Come along, follow me. Come along, shadow."

Kangaroo Joey hopped and plopped, and the shadow slid along and stopped.

When Joey ate his dinner, and rested, the shadow lay on the ground beside him.

Then Kangaroo Joey hopped again. Hop and plop. Slide and stop. All day long he and his shadow moved across the sunlit grass.

Kangaroo Mother called: "Time to go home! You and your shadow must go to sleep."

Then Kangaroo Mother and Kangaroo Joey set off side by side towards home, with their very own shadows, one big, one small.

THE POBBLE
WHO HAS NO TOES

The Pobble who has no toes
    Had once as many as we;
When they said, "Some day you may lose them all;" –
He replied, – "Fish fiddle de-dee!"
And his Aunt Jobiska made him drink,
Lavender water tinged with pink,
For she said, "The World in general knows
There's nothing so good for a Pobble's toes!"

The Pobble who has no toes,
Swam across the Bristol Channel;
But before he set out he wrapped his nose,
In a piece of scarlet flannel.
For his Aunt Jobiska said, "No harm
Can come to his toes if his nose is warm;
And it's perfectly known that a Pobble's toes
Are safe, – provided he minds his nose."

143

The Pobble swam fast and well,
And when boats or ships came near him
He tinkledy-blinkledy-winkled a bell,
So that all the world could hear him.
And all the Sailors and Admirals cried,
When they saw him nearing the further side, –
"He has gone to fish, for his Aunt Jobiska's
Runcible Cat with crimson whiskers!"

But before he touched the shore,
The shore of the Bristol Channel,
A sea-green Porpoise carried away
His wrapper of scarlet flannel.
And when he came to observe his feet,
Formerly garnished with toes so neat,
His face at once became forlorn
On perceiving that all his toes were gone!

And nobody ever knew
From that dark day to the present,
Whoso had taken the Pobble's toes,
In a manner so far from pleasant.
Whether the shrimps or crawfish grey,
Or crafty Mermaids stole them away –
Nobody knew; and nobody knows
How the Pobble was robbed of his twice five toes!

The Pobble who has no toes
Was placed in a friendly Bark,
And they rowed him back, and carried him up,
To his Aunt Jobiska's Park.
And she made him a feast at his earnest wish
Of eggs and buttercups fried with fish; –
And she said, – "It's a fact the whole world knows,
That Pobbles are happier without their toes."

The Frogs Who Wanted A King

Once upon a time, a great family of frogs lived as happily as could be in a green, marshy swamp. It was the perfect place for them. They could splash and leap about with no one and nothing to bother them. There was plenty of food and everything else they wanted for a good life.

But one day, some of the frogs thought that there was something missing from their pond. They wanted to have a king and a proper government. They called a great meeting and agreed to send a message to the great god Jove to ask him to give them what they wanted.

"Mighty Jove," the frogs cried in their croaky voices, "send us a king who will rule over us and keep us in order."

Jove looked down from on high when he heard them croaking. He listened to what they were saying and thought how silly they were to want a king when they already had such a good life. He looked around and saw a huge log lying on the ground. He heaved it up and threw it down into the swamp.

146

All the frogs were frightened out of their wits. They rushed away, swimming as fast as they could, and then turned, trembling, to look at the horrible monster.

The huge log lay in the water with ripples spreading out from it in all directions.

"Greetings, King Log," croaked one of the frogs who had asked Jove for a king.

But King Log lay there silently and never moved. It never spoke to the frogs or told them what to do.

After a time, one or two of the braver frogs crept out towards the log. They swam all around it and looked at it from every side.

One of the younger, more cheeky, frogs swam right up to King Log. She stretched out one foot and touched it. Then she swam away at great speed.

But King Log did not stir.

After a few days, the frogs grew quite used to having King Log lying in the middle of their swamp. They swam round the log without even thinking about it.

Then, one day, the greatest hero of the frogs jumped up onto the huge log. He started to jump up and down on it, croaking, "Look at me! Look at me!"

The other frogs watched with great interest. But nothing happened. Huge King Log did nothing and said nothing. So, one by one, all the frogs climbed onto the log and danced up and down on it.

After that day, the frogs ignored King Log. Sometimes they jumped up on it and sat in the sun. The big frogs taught the little frogs to dive off it into the water.

But the frogs who had wanted the great god Jove to send them a king were not happy.

"King Log is not a proper king," they said. "He's not a king at all." So they called again to the great god Jove.

"Mighty Jove," they croaked, "we want a real king. We want a king that will really rule over us."

Now when Jove heard what they were croaking, he was angry. He thought the frogs were foolish and he decided to teach them a lesson, so he called a great heron out of the sky.

"Heron," he said, "go to the green, marshy swamp where the frogs live and become their king. Rule over the frogs properly, for that is what they want."

So the heron swooped down to the marshy swamp. He stood near the bank with his long legs in the water and, whenever a frog came within reach, he gobbled it up.

"That's a real king," whispered the frightened frogs to each other as they huddled in their homes.

"We were better off with King Log or with no king at all," said the greatest hero of the frogs.

But by then it was too late.

WAKE UP, BEAR...
IT'S CHRISTMAS!

As the last few leaves of autumn fell, Bear was padding down his walking trail. He was going home for his winter's sleep. But he wasn't going to be sleeping all winter.

"That's right," he said, as he reached his door. "I've missed it now for seven years, and seems I've heard it said that it's a happy, joyful time, but always I'm in bed. Well, this year things are different. I've decided what to do. I'm getting up for Christmas, instead of sleeping through!"

After setting his clock and fixing his bed, Bear blew out the candle. Feeling happy but tired, he snuggled down under his blanket.

"Well," he yawned, "when I wake up I wonder what I'll see. Anyway, I hope it's fun when Christmas comes to..."
He fell asleep.

The weeks went by. The forest was still and silent. The only sound was the wind as it blew softly during the day, and harder at night.

The snow started to fall late one afternoon. It fell gently at first, then became heavier. Soon, snow covered nearly everything in the forest. It almost came up to Bear's window.

Bear slept.

The clock woke him late one wintry afternoon. Sitting up slowly, Bear rubbed his eyes. Then he remembered it was Christmas Eve! His nose was cold as he smelled the fresh snow.

Putting on his scarf and mittens, he went out into the woods, where he found a nice little pine tree. Back home in the candlelight, he decorated his tree. He got an old stocking from his cupboard, and hung it up by his window. Then humming a little tune, Bear fixed his blanket and sat back with his guitar to enjoy the evening.

"There. Everything looks cosy now, and festive, I believe. I'm so glad I'm wide awake tonight, on Christmas Eve."

He had not been sitting long when he heard a tapping sound at his door. Just a branch in the winter wind, he thought. But then he heard it again. It was a knock. Before Bear could move, the door opened.

"Hello, Bear. I saw your light. I'll warm myself, if that's all right?"

Delighted by this unexpected visitor, Bear got up and invited him in.

"Well, hello stranger, come on in. Don't stand out there and freeze. It's warm inside and you can rest – here, take my blanket, please. I'm only playing my guitar and looking at my tree. But if you've nowhere else to go, do spend some time with me."

So they sat, Bear and his visitor, talking about the snow and the wind, singing a few tunes, and enjoying Christmas Eve.

Finally, the little fellow, who was now quite warm, stood and said he really must be going.

"I thank you, Bear, for all you've done. This really has been lots of fun."

Bear stood in the doorway and watched him go off through the forest, thinking what a nice time it had been. All of a sudden his friend shouted back at him.

"Come for a ride, Bear, come with me. I'd really like your company."

A ride! On Christmas Eve! Bear grabbed his scarf and mittens and ran through the deep snow to where a big sleigh sat waiting. The little driver turned as Bear reached the sleigh.

"Just climb up here and hang on tight. You'll be back home before it's light."

Wrapping the big quilt around him, Bear sat down in the seat. Before he could say "LET'S BE OFF", they were off!

Off and up! Up through the air and away into the snowy night...

"Oh, what a Christmas!" hollered Bear. "I've never had such fun. I'd like to think that it could be like this for everyone. But most of all, just meeting you has really brought me cheer. Why don't we plan, my little friend, to do this every year?"

So off they flew, far in the night and through the swirling snow, with Bear's companion laughing loud a jolly HO HO HO!

ONE
AT A TIME

Many years ago, there lived a poor man who had an only son. One day, the man realized that there was no more money or food left in the house, so he said, "My son, you must go into the world, find some work and earn some money."

So the young man left home. He walked many miles until he met a rich farmer who had hundreds and thousands of sheep. He needed a shepherd to look after them all, so he gave the young man the job.

There were seven mountains round the farm and there were sheep eating grass in every field on every mountainside. One day, black clouds gathered and there was a storm. Crash, bang! The thunder roared and the lightning flashed. The wind tore off branches and blew down mighty trees. The rain poured down. Streams and rivers overflowed and covered the fields with water. Paths and bridges were washed away.

155

The young man rushed around, gathering the sheep from the seven hillsides to lead them to shelter in the farm. He had almost reached the farm with his enormous flock when he discovered that the bridge over the last stream had been washed away. There was only a wooden plank left, and that was already beginning to break up.

It was only safe for the sheep to walk across the plank one at a time. They did not like the look of the narrow, creaky piece of wood, but the shepherd pushed a big black sheep across and the rest started to follow, one at a time, one at a time.

What happened next? I'll tell you when all the sheep are safely across the plank. At the moment they are still going over, one at a time, one at a time, one at a time.

Have all the sheep crossed over the bridge yet? Oh dear me, no. The young man saved hundreds and thousands of sheep from the mountains and fields. They all have to get across that shaky, rickety plank and they are still crossing over, one at a time, one at a time.

When will the last sheep have crossed, you may well ask? The answer is, they will all have crossed when every single sheep is on the other side! But just now, they are still walking over, one at a time, one at a time.

And what about the young man? Well, he is still waiting, and watching those sheep crossing the plank, one at a time.

One at a time...one at a time.